38481
9-21-95

Dvv   935

D1253332

A Cold Fire Burning

Burning

by Nathan Heard

SIMON AND SCHUSTER / NEW YORK

PS
3558
.E25
C65
1974

Copyright © 1974 by Nathan C. Heard
All rights reserved
including the right of reproduction
in whole or in part in any form
Published by Simon and Schuster
Rockefeller Center, 630 Fifth Avenue
New York, New York 10020

SBN 671-27120-2
Library of Congress Catalog Card Number: 73-20548
Designed by Irving Perkins
Manufactured in the United States of America

1   2   3   4   5   6   7   8   9   10

Introduction

IF ANYBODY were to ask me what were two of the most important and exciting novels today, honesty would compel me to reply: *To Reach a Dream* and *A Cold Fire Burning*, both by Nathan C. Heard. Heard becomes a more exciting novelist book by book. His writing is always graphic and smooth-flowing; each book transcends the previous one. And this is no mediocre achievement when one considers the fact that his first literary effort was most exceptional.

In *Howard Street* there were indications of a great author who could portray such profound pathos in his characters that a reader sensed the reincarnation of Richard Wright and a nightmarish William Faulkner of the American ghetto. These promises have been fulfilled. There was also in Heard's debut novel the blossoming of a unique dexterity in handling the idiom of the modern black ghetto. In *A Cold Fire Burning*, the reader has the rare sensation of seeing this come full flower.

There are very few, if any, writers in the entire country who can handle the continuously evolving dialect of blacks with Heard's accuracy and facility. One gets the impression that this author could accurately predict how an offspring from immigrating Chinese parents would pronounce *piss-pot, poor-ass* or *po-lice*. Heard has an unusually perceptive inner ear for dialect. If his books contained only this virtue, it would be sufficient reason for reading, but this is only one of the numerous priceless qualities of a Heard novel.

A Cold Fire Burning is a fierce and daringly written novel. It is inconceivable that anyone other than Nathan Heard would even attempt such an audacious feat in these times. He probes the psyche of the young black with a deftness and complete absence of inhibition that no other modern writer has exhibited. The author asks some agonizingly penetrating questions about present-day afflictions, questions that have gone unanswered for too long a time. He provides answers. He also analyzes some of the critical ghetto problems and makes provocative statements on the actual legitimacy of the problems themselves.

Heard's evolution into a greater and greater literary figure from book to book is an exciting experience for any reader to share, so much so that the reader honestly dreads the possibility of missing even one of his novels, for fear that he will miss a most significant epoch in the history of American literature—an epoch which can be designated the Next Phase of Literary Evolution of Nathan Heard, who undoubtedly has appeared as the most rapidly maturing talent on the contemporary American scene.

Heard would experience no difficulty whatever in capturing first prize as the modern novelist least dependent on clichés and

6

the one who offers the most imaginative metaphors and literary allusions. He seems to have a real gift for summoning the perfect images when he needs them.

All the characters in *A Cold Fire Burning* are much more human than most of the people any reader knows. Their emotional and moral imperfections and frailties are so credibly proportioned that immediately after one's introduction one senses a lifelong relationship with each of them. Heard's intimate familiarity with the streets combines with a natural ability to analyze, dissect and reconstruct the human personality without misplacing a single molecule. It allows him to portray his characters so vividly that a reader virtually *smells* them for weeks, long after he has put the book down.

This book will in all probability be Nathan Heard's crowning achievement at this point in his career. This novel will also excite curiosity in new readers about his other novels. *A Cold Fire Burning* will motivate professors of liberal arts to include Heard's novels in their syllabi of recommended reading. This book is going to cause a great discovery in America, just as *Herzog* did, just as *Notes of a Native Son* did, and just as *Native Son* did. *A Cold Fire Burning* will cause Americans to discover a great natural resource, Nathan C. Heard, all over again.

CLAUDE BROWN,
author of *Manchild
in the Promised Land*

1

I'M CONSTANTLY thinking that there was never a time when I didn't know that Terri would leave me, that death would be my only avenue of escape. A Voodoo woman once explained that Terri had put a spell on me. She said Terri peed on her hands, then cooked a meal for me, and from that moment on I was under her power.

I don't understand. I don't believe.

Some people say that a man can't know a woman, that it's impossible because she has too many hiding places that are inviolate, or indeed unattractive, and therefore she doesn't want him to look. Maybe so, but I loved her, really and truly, even if she was white.

It didn't matter to me. We made love and talked through

the haze of smoke, the glasses of wine, and the weird scent of sex in my room, which was lighted by the crimson glow of a lone red bulb.

Sometimes in fact I think that the bulb constituted the real measure of our love for each other. Under that bulb in my two-room flat she didn't seem quite so white, nor myself quite so black—not with the wars going on around us, inside us, where murder was a very real act of orgasm, and people wanted to kill for their own precious relief.

But don't get the impression that our love was a solemn affair. Terri had a flair for living. She knew all the good things in life, and she had a drive that caught up others in its enthusiasm and carried them along in its wake without the slightest objection on their part. She was the only person I've ever known who genuinely *loved* everybody.

I suppose that's how we met. I saved her from a hairy situation into which her "friend to man" attitude had cast her. She was on the verge of being ripped-off by some young brothers in the slums of Newark, where she worked in one of the drug abuse programs.

Yeah, I'll never forget the looks of utter incredulity on the brothers' faces when, as they jammed her up against the raw plank construction fence surrounding a vacant lot, feeling all over her tender body, she said:

"I understand why you're doing this. I know your rage and anger. I wish you wouldn't. I wish you'd think why you're doing this thing to me."

They thought she was a nut. She was so calm. No yells, cries or screams. Just gentle words of understanding. When the brothers recovered from her velvet defense, one laughed nervously and countered:

"We know why we doin it, baby—you got a pussy and we wanna fuck. Ain't no better reason."

Can you dig it? I was on my way home from work at the

sewing-machine factory. It was around six in the evening—and I always took a shortcut through that dark little street—when I came upon this scene. The brothers saw me coming, but paid little attention since I very definitely didn't look like a cop or someone who'd interfere. As a matter of fact I didn't intend to interfere, but when I got a better look at Terri I actually felt forced to say something.

I mean, if a word could stop a crime why not say it? Ain't that what the United Nations and world peace are all about?

Anyway, I said, "What you cats doin, man?"

"Gittin some white pussy. It's part of the revolutionary process."

That was Cootie speaking. He spoke so matter-of-factly that I almost continued on my way. I mean, the dude almost convinced my tired brain of his logic. I knew all of them, too. They'd once belonged to the Black Panther Party, then to the Committee for a Unified New Ark, but had been kicked out of both organizations and so formed their own little neighborhood revolutionary cadre made up of themselves and specializing in "touch-off" and "stick-up" tactics, i.e., liberating legal tender. Anyone who opposed them, of course, was part of the oppressive, capitalist, racist, fascist Establishment —and fair game for the revolution.

Anyway, I stopped. "Listen," I said. "Whyn't y'all be cool? I know this chick, she been doin some good things. Ain't no need to rip her off."

Mojo, who was their leader, said, "She gittin ready to do some more good right now for the vanguard of the community lumpen proletariat."

"By gittin raped?" I challenged.

"This ain't rape. This is an obligation of women and part of their contribution to the revolution. We givin her some true revolutionary spirit."

Mojo looked dead serious and Cootie was taking off his

pants while the other two, Sam and Ahmad, held Terri and continued to feel all over her. In fact, I myself couldn't help but notice that she had some fine white thighs. Matter of fact, they looked so good that I momentarily toyed with the idea of joining the revolutionary movement. But these guys knew me and didn't like me and probably wouldn't let me anyway. And then I looked at Terri, at her open, beseeching, trust-filled face. I knew I wouldn't have any part of it. It would be like raping the Virgin Mary, or the all-loving Joan Baez, who'd probably be apologetic for your inner anguish and sing "We Shall Overcome" all the while you were ripping her off.

"Mojo," I said. "How you gon justify revolution by rapin this chick, man?"

Mojo, who was a big, rough-looking guy with a full beard, said, "We don't have to. Brother Eldridge Cleaver did it for us in *Soul on Ice*."

"I ain't gon let y'all do this, Mojo," I said. "And, Cootie, you might as well pull your pants right back up. This pussy ain't for takin."

I saw them tense up, giving me evil eyes, making my spine run tingly with mixed fear and anger. I could see myself, after they'd finished with me, lying in a lake of my own blood: throat cut, stomach ripped open, eyes gouged out, and my right hand severed and stuffed into my big mouth.

I kept thinking I oughta mind my own business.

Finally Mojo said: "You want a revolutionary ass-kickin, man?"

"No, I don't," I replied. "But I ain't backin down." Then my anger grew larger than my fear. I reached into my pocket and felt the cool, hard reassurance of my knife. "If y'all think a piece of white pussy is worth dyin for then come kick my ass, but remember, muthafucka, you gotta *bring* ass to *git* ass —and I'm takin at least two of y'all with me!"

12

Well, to make a long story short, they did let her go after they realized I wasn't jiving and their threats failed to alter my stand. Besides, Sam and Ahmad were in need of a fix, and dope to a junkie is better than pussy. So we departed our battleground in a damn near amiable mood, after I "loaned" them ten dollars to help the cause of the revolution.

It was when we were walking up Springfield Avenue that Terri offered her thanks to me. "I was really frightened," she said.

"You handled it well, I thought."

"Well," she said. "I'd always been told to try not to panic if something like that ever did happen. I never believed it would happen to me. I've been working in this area for a year and that's the first time I've ever felt really afraid."

"What's the name of that organization you work for?" I asked.

"Jump-Off House."

"You always leave there alone?" I was beginning to wonder if she wasn't really looking forward to being raped.

"Not always, but most of the time I do."

"You oughta git you a car. Sometimes it ain't too cool around here for a black woman, much less a white one. Them guys mad at white people, y'know."

"They have a right to be," she said. "I'm mad at them myself."

I watched her from the side of my eyes. She wasn't all that pretty; I mean, she wasn't ugly either, but she wasn't all that pretty. However, she had a really outasight body, and her behind was almost like a sister's. It wasn't flat like most white behinds seem to be. She had long, ash-blond hair. Worn real casual. She sort of reminded me of Sandy Dennis. I guess I was getting a scheme together in my head because we walked in silence for about a block while I thought up something to keep her in my presence.

13

Finally I said, "Whyn't you have your boyfriend pick you up or somethin?"

And then she answered, "I don't have one—a steady one, that is."

Man! When I heard that, visions of those white thighs shot to the center of my brain. I remembered how good they looked. I hadn't had any sex for a while and my groin was speaking to me.

But I was cool.

"I ain't tryin to be smart or anything," I said real calmlike, "but would you like to stop up to my place for a drink? I only live two blocks away." I felt sure she was going to shine me on. You know, like, later for that shit, big boy. But she merely nodded her head and walked along with me.

It seemed like instant magic the way this babe was pulling at my insides. I mean, yeah, I wanted to get her in bed. I was digging her. But this feeling transcended that. The way she talked—soft tones, gentle modulations, sweet easy figures of speech.

And by the time we reached my front door, I knew quite a lot about her background. I knew about her father who was a corporate exec with US Steel, her brother who went to Rutgers Law School. I learned how she deplored their comfortable yet empty existence, and how she had struck out on her own and wanted "to help."

"I wanted to do something," she said at one point. "Can you understand it? *Do something!*"

Sure, I understood.

Of course, my own background was classic—slums, no father in evidence, high school rip-offs, dropouts, hanging-outs, and now a robot on a factory assembly line. Yeah, I understood it. There was little likelihood that my economic status would ever change, that I'd want to hit some dirty ghetto street and "do something." I knew it all the time we walked up those rickety stairs and into my pad, me leading the way because the hallway was so dark, creaky and scary.

I let her in, took her coat and folded it carefully across the back of a kitchen chair while she sat on my sofa bed. "I ain't got nothin but wine," I said.

She smiled. "That'll be fine."

"I keep it in the icebox, so it's cold even if it ain't expensive."

She just nodded. I noticed the way her hair kind of flung itself around her neck and strands of it slapped at her cheeks. It was turning me on. She had such a graceful way of putting it back in place again. It seemed beautiful to me. Her hands simply floated up alongside her face and flicked it back to where it was supposed to be. Even stubby fingers with nails bitten down to the quick couldn't have detracted from the beauty of that hair being tossed back.

I sat a jug of Boone's Farm on the kitchen table and poured out two full glasses for us. I was nervous and spilled a little on myself as I sat down next to her.

"Why you work in the program?" I finally asked.

"Something has to be done. There's no sense to life if we can't do something."

"Yeah," I said, "but with junkies? They want sympathy and handouts. That's why so many of 'em go back on stuff."

She gave me a funny look, like I was crazy, so I asked, a little irritated, "You ever used stuff?"

She shook her head, and said, "No."

"Kinda odd, ain't it?"

She fixed me with a long, hard look. "What do you mean, odd?"

"Well, I mean, why you interested? Them cats is turning on, getting down with it, and you don't even dig what they doin."

This seemed to shake her, so right then I decided to drop

it. Besides I wasn't much interested in dope fiends. "Hey baby," I said, "I guess you right. What kinda music you like?"

She didn't want to get off the drug subject, but after a hesitant moment her features relaxed and she said, "I listen to everything from Bach to Dylan."

"I like James Brown," I said. "He got soul." She just smiled, so I went on: "I got some of his sides here—you wanna hear 'em?"

"Sure," she replied pleasantly.

I got her some more juice first, then put on five "Soul Brother Number One" sides. When the music began I just couldn't keep still. I mean, like it really put me into a thing. I didn't even ask if she knew how to dance; I figured if she was into the black community the way she seemed to be (what with coming up to a black cat's pad and all) then dancing she *had* to know, was a prerequisite to her entry. I grabbed her hand and sure enough this chick had ripped off every dance in the black world, including a couple I wasn't even hip to. I began to admire this babe.

A slow number came on and I rose to my full stature as we began to slow-drag, I mean, really grind it up, man. She was down with that too. The grind is a classic in ghettos. Dances come and go, but the grind never leaves. It's a sexual dance, a kind of dry-fucking. And if a chick does it with a cat alone, in his pad, and feels his johnson getting hard against her thigh, and doesn't stop him, she knows that there's only one place for the dance to end—in bed. I wondered as we danced if she knew; and hoped that she wasn't a tease, or that this whole bit wasn't some sort of patronizing for which I'd be forced to knock her on her ass and kick her out of my place.

But I didn't think she was like that. This girl had paid some dues. She had gotten soul from somewhere, even if she didn't wear it as naturally as a sister could. I'm trying to say that she was a bit stiff at times, but all in all, she was cool. I held her tight. She felt good to me. Soft. I'd never held a white woman like this before. Things happened to me. I tried to be cool, but I was sweating from the effort to maintain it. Visions of *Playboy*'s centerfold blasted my mind. I thought of Raquel Welch, Ali MacGraw and other white movie stars after whom I'd lusted. Baby, I was on a trip! All those wet dreams were come true! In my arms Terri became all the stars everywhere by virtue of her white skin and long, thin hair. Man, I was grooving and didn't need any more wine. This chick had my high in the malleable tenderness of her white arms, which held my quivering body; in the long stretch of her thigh against mine and in the stubby fingers, which toyed with the back of my neck. No way in hell for me to keep my johnson from getting hard. Finally I didn't try to. I knew she felt it. She had to know.

I was so busy with my own reactions that I was mildly shocked when her breathing told me that she was feeling groovy, too. I mean, like it almost floored me to realize that Terri was into a thing of her own, like *ready.* Can you dig it? This was a sho-nuff *white* woman! I mean, *dig it.* I knew I was going to fuck me a white woman. She was giving it to me. I kissed her then, half-expecting her to turn away. She didn't and I kissed her again. Her nose was kind of long—not too long—and I had to kind of find a way around it. But once that awkward moment had passed and we settled into a more comfortable position, that kiss turned out to be one of the best things to happen since Jesus made corporal.

Now her breathing really deepened, and mine along with it. My shock mellowed into a nice, even surprise. *She was accepting me!* I caressed her behind, the meaty part, which was low-slung and soft as foam rubber. There was real substance to her behind and I probed for it with great happiness bub-

17

bling up from the center of my chest. Soon my hands went wild on her, and I was feeling as if to assure myself that she was indeed real.

"Oh!" she sighed. "Oh, Shadow!"

For some strange reason the sound of my name being whispered by her with such desperation shocked me again. I jammed my tongue into her mouth to still the effect so that the memory could linger at length in my mind before she broke the spell again with real words. The kiss ended and a resurgence of passion wound thickly throughout my body as she moaned and again called my soul to attention.

"Terri," I said. "Terri, Terri, baby!"

I didn't pull the sofa bed out. It would have taken too much time. I put the pillows on the floor and laid her down. I took off her clothes. Undressing her fulfilled a lifelong dream of mine—to slowly remove every stitch of cloth that kept me from seeing that elusive, awesome whiteness that had lived somewhere in the back of my mind since I could remember. I was amazed at the contrasts our bodies made. I had to see, to touch her everywhere. I had to smell her, find her essence. I felt funny. I wanted to giggle. It was all so new (just as if I had never seen a naked woman before). It seemed unreal, yet here she lay, my white goddess, stretched out before my hungry soul like a sweet marshmallow. I touched her pussy. It was wet and the thin hairs around it hid nothing from my anxious view. I looked closer, opening those red lips to peer into the quick of her. White moisture formed and trickled down, and I was hypnotized.

I looked into her face as I gently put my finger between those pussylips. Her eyes stared upward and her tongue darted over her lips, which didn't seem to have the ability to stay closed. Then her hand moved to grasp at my johnson. I watched, flabbergasted, throbbing with desire and anticipation, watching her hand, glowing orange in the bulb's crimson light, gripping my hard, black dick. I kept watching. It seemed so essential for me to see everything. I couldn't enter her before I'd seen all there was to see.

Finally she groaned far back in her throat and pulled me toward her. When my johnson first touched her pussy she gave a small squeal and then quickly shoved it in so that my balls banged against her buttocks. Her hands clutched my waist and her legs wrapped themselves around mine. She seemed to be trying to get my whole body inside of hers.

And then all of a sudden my johnson, which a second ago had been threatening to tear her asunder, went limp.

The muthafucka just went *bloop* on me.

I was inside, yes, but the mindless bastard was as lifeless as a withered old tit.

"Goddammit!" I cried in rage and frustration. Terri was so wet, coming left and right, that she didn't even notice what had happened to me.

Moments later, in ignorance, she asked: "What's the matter?"

I was dying! That's what the matter was, wanting desperately to regain my hard. "Nothin, baby," I said. "It's just that you feel so good to me."

This seemed to satisfy her and she went back to taking care of her thing while I fantasized about what I'd do to her when the full power of my eight inches returned. I knew from experience that I'd never get hard so long as she stayed so sloppily wet. The only thing would be to take myself out of her, dry us both off, and let the friction of her pussywalls stimulate my johnson enough for a resurrection. I waited till she had come and come and come, then I eased out my piece of flab and lay beside her pretending that I'd had a natural ball.

Terri got up and went into my toilet while I opened the

sofa to full size and lay there contemplating the red glow of my bulb upon the ceiling and shabby walls. The room appeared to be soaked with blood. The gurgling of the commode being flushed was like the death throes of some great gurgling monster.

Suddenly I was daydreaming of guilt and destruction. In my mind I saw Cootie, Ahmad, Mojo and Sam running wildly down the city streets with bloodstained swords in their hands. They were being followed by great multitudes of black people, all with swords, jabbing, chopping, cutting off blond heads. The screams of men, women and children rang in my ears and I couldn't stop the terrible noise. Then they were coming after me. I couldn't move so they moved over me and chopped off my arms and legs.

I heard Mojo laugh, *"I told you, nigga!"* as he saved my head for last. He was bringing his sword down on me as Terri opened the bathroom door and let her whiteness dissipate the entire scene.

Immediately she began kissing me and feeling me all over as if she knew how badly I needed her touch, and I began to feel real good. I felt very powerful despite the fact that I hadn't shot my seed into her and taken full possession. I mean, right here next to me was an honest-to-god *white* woman! Can you dig it? *A white woman.* I could understand what Ahmad had meant when he said that a nigger would never know the feeling of being a real man until he had fucked the oppressor's woman. I felt whole. Like, man, there would be nothing I couldn't do from now on, if you know what I mean.

Terri put her mouth on my johnson. I felt the warmth of her breath on my stomach and I reacted immediately. My johnson fairly leaped to attention. As fine as it was, however, I didn't want to come anyplace except smack in the middle of her pussy. I eased it out of her mouth, which she seemed reluctant for me to do, and placed myself between those big luscious thighs. Oh, man, it was something else! I mean, she moved so nicely as I went into her. I knew plenty of sisters who could outfuck her, but can you dig it, this was white!

I really socked it to her. I manipulated her into five different positions and she almost blew her mind. My fingers found it hard to grip her buttocks, because of the heavy flow of her orgasms. Finally I settled down for that devastating ride home myself. I had pleasured her to the utmost and it was now my turn. I hunkered in, probing deep and ready for the ultimate thrill. I stroked her long, then short and quick, and felt that first little tingle on my toes that told me I was on my way.

She was getting soaked with my sweat. She moaned and grasped me and seemed out of breath. Still I stroked, still I gave her every fiber a thorough going over, still I pumped and gyrated on her, writhing and twisting in the fires of her lust. And still my little tingle stayed centered around my toes, not working its way up my legs and down from the back of my neck, as it was so accustomed to doing. I thought nothing of it for a while, but as I tried harder and it still refused to budge, I became slightly miffed, which of course broke my concentration. Suddenly the focus of my lust was detaching too, dispersing, breaking loose, and now our coupling was no longer even part of us but something separate, apart, remote as stellar connections. The pleasure was fast becoming a chore.

And on top of that, I looked into Terri's face and saw that she, every now and then, winced. I knew she was probably getting sore. The juices that ran so freely moments ago were drying up, and the friction was causing pain.

I couldn't come! I was cursing myself, writhing in the coils of my own passion. I was hoping against hope that the dying sparks of desire would reignite, burst into flame, and burn their implacable way into a beautiful ending.

But no.

There was nothing but the will, and even that was fast fading.

At length, when I realized that there would be no coming for me, I kissed her as tenderly as I could, and slowly eased myself out of her. Even then she winced in slight pain. I lay on my back and she lay in my arms. The room was heavy with our mingled scents and the red glow glistened off our moist bodies. I could think of nothing to say. There was nothing for me to say.

She stayed at my place until about three in the morning. We talked, but not much. I don't know if she was aware that I hadn't come. At least, she gave no indication of knowing. I hoped she didn't feel any guilt, because the fault had to be mine. It had to be. It was like a prostitute named Johnnie Mae telling me one time about a trick she'd had who couldn't come. She pushed him away and he'd complained.

"Look, man," she told him. "It ain't my fault. The pussy was there and ready. Now go home to yo wife and cry."

But Terri wasn't no whore. She was considerate. She didn't even want me to get up and walk her to the taxi stand just down the block from my pad. So I took her there anyway. The thought of her meeting Cootie or Ahmad was too much.

We made plans to see each other the next day. I would pick her up from work, since I got off earlier than she did. I fell asleep as soon as I got back, and had a dreamless night.

2

MAN, I wish I could explain how truly wonderful I felt at work the following day. I mean, as dull and boring as my job is I didn't mind doing it at all. Everything was cool. My bologna sandwiches tasted like steak, medium rare, right off the grill.

My enthusiasm must have been showing because all day long people kept asking why I was smiling. Most of the time I hadn't realized I had been. I just can't fully express the way I felt. I looked at my fellow workers, especially the white ones, and wondered if they somehow could tell what I'd done last night. I know it was a foolish thought, but I wanted to know how they would react to me now that I had had a white woman—I mean, I was almost one of them, almost.

I was a club member!

I also puzzled over their drab, hard faces. Like, they ought to have been happy all the time because they had white women all the time. I knew their powerful strength now. I wanted so badly to tell them, just throw it up in their faces, let them know that I knew where they were at.

But I didn't say anything to anyone. I worked hard and gladly, and before long it was time to knock off and go home. Go home? Hah! It was time to go get my woman!

Anyway, when I reached the storefront office of Jump-Off House she was standing in front waiting for me. Dig it—*waiting for me!* I slowed my pace when I saw her. After all, even though I'd been damn near running to get there, I had to maintain my cool; besides, there were people around, digging her, and I wanted them to see the way I intended to ease up to her and stroll away with her on my arm.

She gave me a big smile. "Hi," she said.

"What's happenin, baby?" I asked, real cool. "Wanna go down to All-Pro and cop a chicken sandwich?"

"I don't mind," she replied. "I love chicken."

All-Pro was only a couple of blocks away so we started out, hand in hand. I was burning to ask her about last night. I mean, like, how she felt about it and all . . . and also if she would be my steady woman. I was thinking that she was thinking that I probably fucked white women all the time, so having her would be no big thing to me. That would be cool and would, I hoped, help me get over with her, but I also didn't want her to think I took her lightly.

"What about last night?" I finally blurted.

"What about it?"

"I mean, what'd you think? I mean, you dig it, or what?" I was becoming angry. It suddenly occurred to me that maybe she didn't think it was a big thing, either. Maybe she had been doing it to other black men. Maybe she wasn't so goddamned exclusive after all. And I don't dig no broad putting me on, black or white.

"Of course I did, Shadow." She gave that easy smile of hers and I was reassured.

I didn't mean to say any more. I really didn't. But I couldn't help myself. The question came out all by itself: "How many other black men you had before me?" I couldn't even look at her.

We had reached the door of All-Pro by now. She stopped and leveled a look at me that I'll never forget, and suddenly I had never in my life felt so instantly guilty.

"Would it matter?" she finally asked. "Why not ask me about the white men I've had, too? Or don't they matter to your prejudiced mind?"

"Hold on there," I bristled. "Damn if I'm prejudiced. I just asked a question for my own information."

"Well, for your information, I've gone out with one other black man, but you're the only one I've gone to bed with. Does that please you?"

To no mean end, it did. But I wasn't about to let her know it. Broads use stuff like that against you.

"It ain't a matter of pleasin me, Terri." I made my voice very convincing. "I want to know all about you, that's all. You please me just by livin, and I believe you gon become very important to me."

She liked that, man. There was that smile of hers again, and with deep sincerity she said, "I'm glad."

I touched her arm. "Would you like to be my woman? I mean, I really dig you, and I'd treat you right . . ."

Right there, in the middle of broad daylight, she kissed me. She didn't care who saw it. I cared, though. I wanted every-body to see that I was down with it, making it, and was into something groovy. I had me some white pussy any time I wanted it. Not many spooks could say that.

We got two sandwiches and I stopped down at *Jackson's Lounge* to buy a jug of Boone's Farm and a six-pack of Bud. I had drunk Bud ever since I'd seen Frank Sinatra do a commercial for them, because I liked the way Sinatra got along with Sammy Davis, Jr.

Terri and I were on our way to my pad when we ran into Mojo, Sam, Ahmad and Cootie. They walked behind us making all sorts of nasty remarks. I released Terri's hand and put mine on my blade inside my pocket; it reassured me that everything was cool.

"Hey, y'all, dig this shit, willya?" Mojo said to his boys. "The bitch done gone and hired a muthafuckin bodyguard!"

Ahmad cracked, "How much she payin you, *house nigga?*"

"She payin him two big fucks a week!" Sam said, and they began to laugh and try to outdo one another's remarks as they walked along behind us.

I didn't mind them so much, but soon other people joined them and some young kids started a chant:

"What you havin f'dinner?"

"Crackers!"

"What you havin f'dessert?"

"Oreo cookies!" Then they laughed and the chants continued to slam at us, over and over again, until Terri was on the verge of tears.

The kids finally dropped off, but Mojo and his boys followed us right onto my block, still agitating and insinuating. I had attempted to turn and face them but Terri stopped me. I decided to make a stand at my stoop. I handed my key and the packages to Terri and sent her upstairs despite her objections. Then I turned to the gang.

"What you muthafuckas think y'all doin?" I demanded.

"We ain't doin a thing, good brother," Ahmad quipped.

"We just walkin down these semifree streets of our little ghetto."

"Why y'all fuckin with me, man?" I was getting hot. "Y'all better find somebody else to mess with."

Mojo moved closer, followed by the others. My hand tightened on my blade.

"You wanted it all for yo'self, huh?" Mojo accused. "Didn't want us to have none at all. That ain't unity, brother."

"That ain't what happened," I said. "I wasn't tryin to do nothin but keep y'all outa trouble."

Sam pointed his finger in my face. "What you doin with her now?"

"She my woman now," I replied.

Ahmad started toward me. His face seemed to crack up into a few hundred pieces. "You a black-assed liar! You a goddamn counterrevolutionary, and we gon off you, punk!"

"You better back up off me," I said. "You want revolution, jus keep fuckin with me and my woman, there's gon be a full-scale war."

"Dig this sucka, willya?" Cootie said. "He ready to die for that bleached bitch."

"That ain't it," I said. "It's jus that y'all can't go around rippin-off everyone who don't agree with y'all. That's all. If you gon do that, why don't y'all start at City Hall or the White House?"

"Because niggas like you stand in our way," Sam said. "You think you protectin yo'self by protectin them."

Mojo put in: "Niggas like you gotta be moved on. You in the way."

"I don't know about movin *on* me," I answered, "but you better damn sure move *away* from me—and I mean it, too. Who the hell is you to judge me?"

"The revolutionary vanguard of the people!" Ahmad retorted. "And you been sentenced to death, nigga!"

"For what?" I asked.

"For bein a traitor," he said. "For fuckin that white bitch for selfish reasons. The people done fixed yo sentence."

"You and the people both can kiss my black ass," I shouted back. "My revolution don't come through the head of my dick. And, furthermore, before you start talkin *for* the people, you oughta start talkin *to* them. They don't seem to think much of y'all in this neighborhood."

Before anyone could move, Sam lunged at me. "You jive-time punk!" he spat.

His fingers clutched my arm. My knife whipped and took a plug from the back of his hand.

"Come on, muthafucka!" I shouted as he fell back. "I'll cut yo ass everywhere but loose if you touch me again."

The others had to grab him because he was coming at me again. "We gon see you around again, nigga," Mojo said as they dragged Sam away.

"You been doin that for years, man," I shot back. "Ain't much sense in me changin turf now."

As they walked away, I was one happy dude. My legs shook so bad as I walked up the stairs that I had to hold onto the banister to keep from falling. I didn't want to tangle with those guys, but a man can't take low when his woman is around. And I was determined that they weren't going to run over me, take my chance at happiness and trample it under their GI surplus boots. After all my years in the neighborhood, why couldn't they let me have my chance? Why did they even think about messing with me? This is where I was born, and where I had every conceivable reason to believe I would die. To me, their ideas about changing things in this country were as rotten and scummy as the Passaic River.

Why should they want to start with me anyway? Who was I? Why was it so important who I fucked? I knew white from black. I mean, like, I'm not a fool, and I'd also had a few dreams, but I do know white from black. Can you dig it? Those guys had to be crazy.

Look—I worked at my job and took life as it came to me. I know, as a black man, that I'll never be completely free in this country, I mean, who is anyway? Despite what the revo-integrationists say. Like, the white guy who works next to me on the job isn't free, either. I couldn't understand Mojo as I can't understand anyone who talks about freedom, justice and equality as though Americans will ever really be ready for real fantasies. Nothing had ever made me as happy as Terri had. In twenty-four hours my blocked juices became a smooth-flowing brook. There came with her a meaning, a sense of fulfillment, you know; the things a man really needs. Who were Mojo, Cootie, Ahmad and Sam to try and take this away from me? Who the hell was anybody?

My thoughts ran deep as I made it up to my pad. Terri saw my confusion and despair for she rushed quickly to my arms, examining me for signs of physical hurt even after I'd told her there had been no contact between the gang and me. She listened closely as I related what had occurred downstairs and by the time I finished we both had lost our appetites.

But we did drink the wine, and as she finally sat her glass down, she said, "Have you ever thought of the possibility that they might be right, Shadow?"

"Is the Pope gon become an Orthodox Muslim tomorrow?" I shot back. "Hell no! I ain't thought about it, and don't intend to. We ain't known each other for a whole day yet; I don't know a damn thing about you, but I know you better than anyone I've ever known. That make sense to you?"

"No it doesn't, but I love it all the same," she said.

We sort of laughed it off then and let the subject drop while we downed the juice. It was beginning to get dark outside, so I finally asked:

"Where you live? Don't you have to go home?"

"I live over on Prospect Street—the heart of honkytown. And if you're asking if someone's waiting for me the answer is no. I have a roommate but we mind our own business."

"Ain't nothing in the world wrong with mindin yo own business," I said. "Is you my sweet baby?"

"Mmmm," she murmured. "Every bit."

"I like the way you answer," I said. "You make a man believe every word you say."

I kind of smiled, drank more of my wine and looked at my alabaster love. Then I was touching her, holding her. She had the power to enchant me and I felt warmly drained of the will to do anything but bathe myself in the sheen of her hair and the glittering incandescence of her open blue eyes. It seemed that she had always had this magical power over me; I felt will-less with her. She had controlled me ever since we'd met; she was all over me and I would never rid myself of her scent, which seemed to hang forever on the itching tip of my nose. This was destiny and fate and God, and touched the most hidden part of my soul.

"I wanna make love to you—now," I said, already standing to get out of my shirt.

"I want you, too, darling," she replied softly.

"Man!" I mean, dig it. Nobody, nowhere at no time had ever called me darling. It was alright in the movies, but I could never say it right myself because it sounded kind of odd —phony, if you know what I mean. Like, that's strictly a white man's word, see? Black people say honey or baby with a lot more ease than they can darling, I think. But when Terri said it to me it sounded like her mouth was just made to speak that word to me. I could even begin to reason out what was going on inside my head; what was happening to my stomach and my shoulders and to the bottom of my feet. Where had my ghetto cool gone to? That intangible thing that made it possible to survive without irreparable damage to one's soul? Nothing, no one had ever so completely gotten to me as had Terri. The idea of her chilled and warmed me, making a balance of too little and too much at one and the same time. I had no complaints, just an unreasoning knot of fear and awe of something I couldn't identify.

Then she had my johnson out and was holding it in her hand. It was so damn natural. She gave a close examination to that hunk of black meat filling her delicate hand and smiled at the bit of secretion that seeped out. She gave out a small cry of joy and kissed it when it jerked of its own volition. I stood weak but boldly in front of her looking down at the top of her head, where her hair parted in the middle and fell to both sides of her face. She was on the couch now, disrobing, my johnson held sweetly in her moist mouth. As she undressed herself, she allowed me to thrill and wonder at her gyrating tongue and lips, at her white and pink loveliness. She tenderly toyed with my hanging balls, which almost ached to rid themselves of sperm. The contrast between our skins startled me, fascinated me. How white she was! I was blinded. Her hands on me were soothing as silk, soft as down. She let her tongue play over me, stroking the sides and bottom and top, every so often blowing her warm breath between my legs. I grew weak with the effort to stand and trembled and felt a high that was unattainable with mere wine. Pressure mounted within me and I had to wrap my hands in her hair, feeling the deepest need to hold onto my sanity that way. She stroked me easily; her mouth resilient and so resourceful. Her hands gently massaged my behind and her finger, from time to time, threatened entry between my buttocks making me stiffen with wonder and a mild curiosity about how it would feel if she would jam it in.

Suddenly, without even a hint of what was happening, I came. I had no warning. It was a strange coming too, one that filled instead of draining me. I had never come like this before. I couldn't savor it for it was there and gone before I had the opportunity to really get down with it. Terri, God bless her, seemed to take all of my johnson into her mouth. I tried to keep my eyes open, to observe that special event, but all I was able to see was blackness spotted in a million places with tiny white dots that turned to a glowing red that set off a ringing in my head. The sensation split my mouth to let out a very loud moan. I grew simultaneously hot and cold, strong and weak, angry and so very, very pleased. When Terri released me I sank to my knees in front of her in utter helplessness. I think I even cried a little as I buried my head in her lap in order to return the joy that she had so preciously given me.

Later, when we lay in bed watching my portable TV, Terri suddenly turned to me and said, "I know this can't last, but while it does let's make the best of it."

Just like that. Out of the clear blue sky. What the hell was she talking about? "It can last," I said. "And it will last. We gon make it work."

"They won't let us—"

"They who?" I asked, my anger rising.

"People. Neither yours nor mine. They'll destroy us or make us destroy ourselves." Tears sparkled her eyes. "I've watched how the attitudes of black people toward me have changed in the year that I've worked here. There are so many more Mojos and Cooties and Ahmads now and their resentment hits me harder each day."

"Hell! That's just talk. Don't worry about it. Let's see what comes of it first—and as far as people destroyin us . . . that can only happen if we let it happen."

She must have felt my confident vibes because she turned and grabbed me like a wild woman. I kissed her face and neck and ears and everything else within reach of my lips. I felt her breasts until they bloomed under my hand and strained for the gentler, moister stroke of my lips and tongue. Soon she relaxed, and soon everything but us was forgotten.

We made love again, but still, the only way I could come was when she put her mouth on me again. It wouldn't have bothered me so much except that after she had left I think she knew. And then when I was alone, I thought about her pussy and jerked-off and was able to come in less than one minute.

It really made me wonder what the hell was going on.

3

I DON'T know anyone in the world who has felt completely free, but I know how I think they ought to feel if they're free, and if there are such people I was one of them; for during the weeks that Terri and I went together I found out what a man ought to feel like. I mean, like a whole new bag opened up for me. It was as if I'd found something that I'd been in desperate search of, something I'd somehow misplaced but knew was somewhere nearby.

And Terri was responsible for it all. I guess the best thing I can say about it is that I wanted to get inside of her, I admired her so very much.

Although I had lived in the shadow of New York City all of my life, I'd never been anywhere more exciting than Coney Island. I'd never been to the observation tower of the Empire State Building, or even to the museum in downtown Newark for that matter. I'd never been near a boat or seen a real baseball game except on television. And, man, to see a real Broadway play had never even crossed my mind. Eating in a restaurant that wasn't a greasy spoon almost gave me a nervous breakdown. With Terri I went skiing once, can you dig it?

Terri took me under her wing, so to speak; she guided me and I was developing an identity with her and the things she liked. We read books together. We went to see some black plays, too. But most of them made me feel kind of messed up, if you know what I mean. Some of them made me feel like I wasn't really supposed to be seeing them with her; the actors reminded me of Mojo and his guys, and sometimes I would look out of the corner of my eyes to see if Terri got the same messages I seemed to be getting.

As a matter of fact one of those black plays was the cause of our first real fight. I've forgotten the name of the play—something like *Black Domain,* written by one of those separationist playwrights who scream rage and pain and curse words at the audience with a subtle underlying plea to white people for a piece of the capitalist action. I guess you could say that the playwright was sort of a Ford Foundation–approved revolutionary.

Anyway, we were on the train coming back to Newark when Terri turned to me and asked, "What did you think of the play, Shadow?"

At the moment I wasn't thinking anything about it but I replied, "The same thing I think about Mojo, Cootie, Ahmad and Sam. They askin people to do things they know damn well ain't gon git done."

She smiled at me in a way I didn't like, as if I were a kid or something. "I think it goes a little deeper than that. Black writers are demanding that people recognize the need for a black esthetic, a black ideal that can't become a reality under a strictly white power structure."

"I don't know about all that," I said. "But I know they talkin about separation. They talkin about replacin what little we got with nothin but a promise. Shit, we had enough promises already."

"That's exactly what I mean." Terri's eyes widened with what looked like real pleasurable excitement to me. "What about when the young warrior said: 'This is what we claim as ours, this land is ours for we have taken it and we will build upon it!' after they got out of the detention camps?"

"They didn't have nothin to claim and nothin to build on —and the white people still had all the power, didn't they?"

"Shadow . . ." she said this very deliberately. "Don't you see? It was implied by the writer that the white power was only temporary. The black people now had more than just empty hope because of the intervention of the Third World countries . . ."

I was getting angry and it showed because I heard my voice rising and felt my throat becoming constricted. "Who the hell gon be fool enough to trust them foreigners? I think they was gittin ready to negotiate them niggas right back into them camps for the release of the Virgin Islands . . ." It burned me to have Terri presume to know more about black folks than I did. I saw a sellout coming in that play, or at least I thought I did. "A black man can't trust no other country as much as he can trust America—and I ain't sayin that America is all that trustworthy, either. But I believe it's the best hope we got right now."

She looked at me as though I were some kind of nut. "You can't be serious."

"How come I can't? I'm damn serious! Why you think all them separatist–revolutionist niggas ain't left here? And don't tell me they tryin to save everybody either. They just know where they got the best chance of shootin off their mouths and stayin alive. They don't want no land of their own, they want

36

color TVs, and Cadillacs and suburbia just like the rest of us —and they stayin right here where they got at least a small chance of gittin 'em."

"I refuse to believe that," Terri said sullenly. "And I really feel odd arguing with you—a black man—about it." She gave a sly smile then: "Y'know, I do believe that you have a little Tom in you."

I don't know what I felt at that precise moment, but before I realized it I had smacked her almost off her seat. I didn't mean it, but neither could I help it. I simply had to do it. She made no outcry or anything. She looked hard at me for a moment and I watched the red mark on her cheek come to an almost glowing brightness. Then she turned, dry-eyed, to the window and stared out until the train pulled into Newark's Penn Station.

"I'll take a taxi—to my apartment," she deliberately declared once we were outside of the station.

"That what you really wanna do?" I asked.

"Very much so. That's exactly what I want to do."

There goes my loving for tonight, I thought to myself. And all evening long I had been looking forward to it. "You mad?" I asked.

"I'm disappointed," she said. "No one has ever hit me before." She stood looking at me and now I could see the silent tears beginning to course down her cheeks, but for that show of emotion she seemed extremely calm.

I was sorry, and seemed to see her sadness, her little-girl helplessness, in a mixed light of pain and sexuality, so much so that my desire for her increased immediately. I wanted to make up.

"You shouldn't have called me an Uncle Tom, honey," I said.

She didn't respond.

"Want me to pick you up from work tomorrow?" I asked.

As much as I wanted her, something kept me from begging her not to go home right now.

"No," she replied. "I have something to do."

"Want me to call you later on?"

Very quietly she said, "I'll call you."

"When?"

"I don't really know. I have to think." She turned and got into the waiting cab. I watched it as it went up Raymond Boulevard.

I wasn't going to take low. I wanted to say I was sorry, but I wasn't going to. She had wronged me first and she hadn't apologized. She could go, I thought. She could go straight to hell.

Yet, even as I thought this, I also knew that I didn't mean it. I was very tempted to hop a cab and follow her. I held myself in check, though, and began to walk up Market Street feeling a great sense of loss. The temptation to follow her persisted. I knew where she lived although I'd never been to her place. She had only invited me once and I had declined. I don't know why, but I felt funny about meeting her roommate; I think I felt funny about meeting anyone connected with the white side of her life. Like, even the times when I'd called and her roommate had answered the phone, I tried to make my voice sound as white as possible. Terri had told me that her roommate knew about me, but, somehow, I wasn't able to deal with the situation. Right now, however, with the loss of her gnawing at my insides, I was tempted to go there and present myself in all my blackness, to kick down the door if need be. She was my woman and I had the right to claim her.

I kept walking up Market Street absently looking at the merchandise secreted behind the barred windows of the many stores; looking at my sorry image between those bars. I stopped once to view myself closely, not knowing what the hell I was looking for. I saw my face distorted by a pair of blue jeans in an Army Surplus store.

The streets were nearly deserted, and I found myself wondering where all the people had gone to, until I remembered that Newark was now a ghetto where only the brave or the foolish walked at night. From four to six in the evening it was impossible to get across Market Street because all the white people were fleeing the city in their cars, doors securely locked and windows rolled tightly up, eyes anxiously trying to watch the traffic and the many black faces outside as well, or trying equally as hard not to watch the faces.

The street was mine and I felt all the aloneness that one must feel on a deserted island; I was a crippled ship listing precariously on a dying sea.

"You gonna buy somethin there, fella?"

I didn't even have to look to know to whom the voice belonged. When I turned I saw the thin, birdlike face and hard eyes of the cop sitting in a patrol car my loneliness vanished into anger because from the tone of his voice he was out to play God tonight.

"Just window-shopping," I said. "Am I breakin a law?"

He spat out of the window. "Move on, buddy. G'wan home and come back tomorra."

"I *am* home," I said sarcastically.

His partner laughed, but Birdface didn't think it was funny at all. "C'mere, fella," he ordered.

I walked over to the car and stood about two feet away. I had no fear, but I was slowly filling with anger at the thought that he could order me around in a voice that was worse than as if he had hit me. "What you want?" I asked.

"Show me some ID."

I pulled out my wallet and gave him my social security card and a few other things with my name and address on them. He deliberately took an exorbitant amount of time looking them over. "Where ya live?" he asked without looking up.

"Right where it says I live on there." I pointed at the papers.

"Then how come ya told me that ya live in front of that store?"

"Look," I said. "I ain't botherin nobody, and I'm a resident of this city. Now why don't y'all just let me go on?"

Birdface turned to his partner. "Is anybody holdin him, Pete?"

"I ain't holdin him," Peter answered. He leaned over to look at me: "Who's holdin ya, pal?"

"Well, gimme back my stuff and let me go," I said.

Birdface said. "That ain't no way to ask for somethin. We're only doin our job. We're protectin you people from muggers. Any prostitutes try to accost ya tonight?"

"Look, man—"

"Look *who?*" Birdface jumped on that.

"Look, officers," I corrected, "ain't nobody botherin me and I ain't botherin nobody. Now why don't y'all—"

"Y'know what?" Birdface said. "I think you're a wise guy. I also think you're a suspicious character. Get in the car while we check you out."

He was getting out of the car and I was backing away. "I ain't done nothin and I ain't gittin in no car," I said.

"He ain't gittin in the car, Pete," Birdface said.

Peter got out of his side. "You gonna resist us?"

"I ain't resistin nothin," I said as they both moved toward me. "I just wanna go home."

"But you're already home, remember? You told us that."

"Leave me alone," I said, desperately looking up and down the deserted street for help.

"And if your home is in the street, then you're a vagrant."

They both had their sticks out. I had backed all the way to

the store window and couldn't go any farther. Pete's face looked stern, but Birdface looked positively happy and I knew that he was going to hit me with that stick, that he wouldn't be satisfied until he had. Frantically I tried to think of something. I didn't know whether I should try to fight or try to run away. But I knew that to run was to chance getting shot. They could easily say I was trying to break into a store. Nobody would even question them. I'd be dead and nobody would even question them. Perhaps, I thought, if I let them get their sadistic kicks it wouldn't be so bad. I was going to get it and there was nothing I could do except take it or die. Still, knowing that there was no way out, I couldn't make myself get into their car. I would only sacrifice myself so far; they could only get a limited amount of cooperation from me in my own sacrifice.

"Get in the car," Birdface ordered.

"No!" I said, and suddenly found myself ducking a hard thrust of his club to my stomach.

"The nigger's fast, Pete," Birdface said.

"All niggers are fast," Pete replied. "But watch this." He feigned a blow at my legs that made me reach down to try and ward it off. But as I did so, he shifted quickly and came with a roundhouse left that caught me on the chin. I was stunned; there were sudden bright flashes of light zinging their way to my brain and the side of my entire body was a mass of stinging pinpricks.

I was lying flat on my back looking up at them before I even realized that I'd been knocked down. Birdface seemed preoccupied with jabbing his club into my stomach while Pete, gratified in his fistic powers, went to work on me with his hands. Since I'd decided not to fight back, I balled myself into a knot and let them have their way.

The beating didn't last long and really didn't hurt that much, but I was crying from the humiliation. Through it all nothing was said. They grunted more than I did and were breathing twice as hard. Finally, when they ceased, Birdface said, "Awright, nigger. You gonna get in the car now?" He could hardly talk.

I didn't say anything, but I shook my head and dodged his foot enough for it to glance off my arm.

"You black sonuvabitch! I oughta killya." Birdface was trembling in his anger. His gun hand twitched as it moved to the gun holster. And I think he just might have shot me if Pete hadn't cooled him by pulling him away.

Birdface threw my papers at me. "All you black bastards think you're smart since ya got that nigger in the mayor's office. But let me clue ya"—he pointed his club at me—"it ain't gonna do ya no goddamn good, y'hear that? It ain't gonna do ya no goddamn good! Ya ain't never gonna run this town. *Never!*" He whacked me across my legs before allowing Pete to lead him back to their patrol car.

I lay on the ground for a while before picking up my papers. I didn't want to get up. I felt that there was never going to be reason for me to ever get up from the ground. I sat there, feeling nothing but despair. The pain inside my body nullified any other. A car went by and I heard, as if from a great distance, someone shout: *"Get up from there, you bum!"* I got up.

By the time I got home, all I could recall with any clarity was the fact that Terri and I had broken up. It was all that mattered. And as drab as my pad, job and life were, and as bad as I felt, nothing was more horrible to me than her absence. I turned on the portable television and stood staring dumbly at the vague flickering images on the screen. I went to the icebox and got my wine, then I sat and began to drink without taste or pleasure.

I couldn't understand what was happening to me. Everything was turned around in my head, senseless. Especially the argument with Terri over the posturings of a foolish writer and his empty words. My brain was so fogged I felt on the verge of nausea. As I downed another glass of wine, I turned off the television and lay down fully dressed on the sofa to stare up at my cracked, sagging ceiling and the crimson glow of the walls and floor.

I knew right away that I would not be able to sleep. Terri's face and her words—that final goodbye—burned into every nook of my sensibility, haunting my consciousness with weird goings-on that led to her leave-taking with the ass-end of the taxi blinking a sneer of "later, chump" at me.

What the hell did she want me to do, join some militant group so that I'd never be able to walk the streets alone again? Though, after my encounter with the cops, being with someone didn't seem like a bad idea. Yet, it was as though she were forcing me between an early grave or jail. The odds in either case were against me.

I wondered as I lay there what was it about people these days that made them spend so much time and energy making sure a man couldn't live his life as he saw fit. How was it I had to wind up defending white people to a white person? Why was race so goddamned important to everybody? Hell, I didn't even know I lived in a ghetto at one time. Who did? I was happy then. We didn't always have what we wanted, but the bliss of our ignorance was that we didn't need very much, and we made the most of that.

Now I increasingly found myself pushed, berated, threatened and beaten for reasons that totally escaped me. I wondered what in the world I'd done. To call myself an American was to be labeled a Tom or house nigger. What am I supposed to be, and how do I prove I'm anything at all?

I was lost meditating on the buckling walls and ragged ceiling, and to lay there much longer would have driven me insane. I sat up and looked at the clock. It was 11:30 P.M. and still early enough to go out and have a few drinks at Spoon's place where niggers act like niggers and everyone's not trying to be saviors.

Spoon's was a small place, consisting of a jukebox, pool table, set in the middle of the room, and a bar with twenty or so wobbly stools. The cigarette machine and the busted pay phone made it seem even more crowded.

And it was crowded when I got there. Five arguments raged around the narrow horseshoe bar, and the jukebox blared its sad, soulful sounds. Half the people that night seemed to be fags. They were dancing and posturing in a corner with agile, feline grace.

It was noisier than a four-alarm fire and it seemed to be the perfect place for me.

Spoon saw me and came over. "My man. What's happ'nin, baby?"

"Just tryin to survive, Spoon," I said.

"Yeah, we all tryin to do that, Jack. Whatcha drinkin?"

"Beer. Any kind." He served me up a cold bottle of Bud, poured out a glass, then drifted down the other side of the bar, leaving me in peace.

The place was dimly lit and the people at the bar were loud and frantic. "The nigga threw the fight, man!" one gestured and sloshed his drink over his hand. "They shoulda kicked his ass outa the Muslims."

His companion pointed a finger at his chest. "You tellin a muthafuckin lie. He didn't throw it. That boy give him a righteous ass-kicking. It was cold, man. There ain't nobody in the world that somebody somewhere can't beat. You just got brainwashed by that nigga's loud mouth."

"Man," the first returned. "I was sittin right there in the movie and Ali was messin around with that cat. I wouldn'ta

44

minded it so much, but the nigga made me lose my *last* twenty-five dollars by fuckin around."

"Listen. I was there too, and . . ."

My ears picked up another conversation.

". . . so I told the bitch, I said: 'Bitch, you ain't puttin *me* out this house. I'll tell the goddamn welfare on yo ass!"

"I know that scared the shit outa her, didn't it?"

"Damn right it did. See, cause I know where she hiding that car she ain't spozed to have. And I also know the name she got that job under too."

"Well, what she do then?"

"Hah! She unpacked my shit and left me the hell alone. That's what she did—and quick, too. I *know* what to do f'one of them bad bitches, man. Don't no whore run me!"

I ordered another beer. When I looked up, a white fag had joined the corner queers and was eyeing me. There was a vague similarity between him and Terri. It was making me feel uneasy. It wasn't like the feeling black fags gave me. He made me long for Terri. I really felt kind of bashful. I was very near to calling her up on the phone and almost ready to beg her to see me.

Other arguments among the customers kept intruding upon my thoughts, and the white fag's face kept getting mixed up with Terri's until I felt that if I didn't get out of Spoon's fast I would either kill him or fuck him, or maybe both. Each, I felt, I could do.

Just as I was preparing to leave, Ahmad walked in fresh from a night of revolutionary rip-offs, and ordered a fifth of Gordon's. Then he saw me. "Hey, Shadow!" he shouted loud enough for everyone to hear. "Where yo white devil woman at?"

"The same place yo revolution is—home in bed," I retorted, bringing peals of laughter from the people in the bar.

Ahmad was decked out in his Afro, jump boots and dashiki.

45

His chest was covered with medallions and bone necklaces, all of it no doubt hot.

And much of it, I thought longingly, could be used to choke him in close combat.

And I was feeling just mean enough to try it too, especially since he was alone, although I'd guessed his boys were waiting outside.

He looked me up and down, a sneer wolfishly curling the corner of his mouth.

"Don't look at me, nigga," I said. "Dig yoself, lookin like a refugee from a Tarzan movie." Again I got the laughs from the crowd.

"You see somethin wrong with traditional dress, *negro?*" He put deliberate emphasis on that last word, knowing that it would sway the crowd back in favor of him.

"Is you African?" I asked. "All that shit you wearin don't make you no African. You still a nigga."

He gave a sudden smile. "It may not make me no African, sucka. But dig this: Robert Hall ain't made you no American either."

The crowd really jumped on his side then. They made me feel so small, and I couldn't think of any jokes or comebacks that would get me back into their grace. And the funny thing is that uppermost in my mind was the concern that the white fag had witnessed my defeat. I don't know how, but it seemed that through him Terri also witnessed it. The others mattered nothing to me because, despite their sympathy to Ahmad, not one of them was dressed like him. They all looked like me, thought like me. I wanted to ask them why they were laughing; if they felt like him why weren't they with him. Instead I got up and walked out of the door. Outside I saw Mojo, Cootie and Sam sitting in an old beat-up car with the motor running, waiting for their partner. I turned and walked in the other direction.

4

I HELD out for almost a week, but only because I stayed drunk and hungover. I don't know how I managed to make it, yet I did. However, I stayed to myself and dodged the comments that were made about how I looked. And I guess I must have gone through whole cases of liquor, beer, and wine. There were empty bottles all over my pad. I spilled so much in bed that my sheets looked like I had fucked five girls on the rag.

It was Thursday morning when I finally came out of my stupor. I cranked my eyes open to gradually let the room come into focus around me. After a bender of the likes I'd had, everything is seen out of focus. I was dying of thirst and very hungry, in fact, I couldn't remember the last time I'd eaten anything. I didn't want to stay in bed and I didn't want to go to work, and I decided to do neither.

After stumbling into the toilet to relieve myself I splashed cold water on my face and dried it with my undershirt. I didn't care if I looked ashy or not so I didn't put any oil on my face. I needed a shave anyway so the ash wouldn't show that much.

I had a strange urge to hurry but I didn't know why I should. There was a near-empty pint of Seagrams on the table. I gagged it down then put on my jacket and left the apartment for the streets. And as soon as the brisk morning air swallowed me I knew that there was nothing, nothing in this entire city waiting for me. What I had felt upstairs was only the need to escape my stinking pad and anywhere I went would be better than where I had been.

It was too early for the bars to be open, but I remembered that the OK pool parlor opened around nine in the morning and it was near that time now. Broadway would let me in even if he wasn't ready to open; he even let some guys sleep there when the weather was too bad for them to cat in cars and hallways. The winter Hawk made philanthropists of the strangest people.

I started toward Prince Street where the pool hall was located. It was the only building left standing on that side of the street: a little square, squat building that seemed to have been slapped together by a one-armed blind man with the DTs. Yet it fit into the neighborhood. It went perfectly with the tenements, projects and bums, the junkies, hookers, hustlers and storefront poverty programs.

Broadway let me in without saying a word and returned to brushing off the tables while chomping on his cigar. I went to the rear table, racked the balls and began shooting eight-ball by myself, hoping to perfect a five-rail bank but hardly able to break.

For over an hour Broadway and I were the only ones in the

place. But soon it began to fill with players and onlookers, who sat on the sideline benches to look, bet or catch a nap. Others sat to wait for a sucker to come in so they could relieve him of his pride as well as his money. Recently a number of junkies had taken to hanging around. Broadway had lately become adept at spotting them and barred them from coming inside except to shoot pool because they had begun using the back of the toilet casing to stash heroin. After a few busts and numerous police raids Broadway kept a wary eye on everyone, to the extent that he'd even accused a few of his well-known customers of nodding from drugs when in fact they had only been catnapping.

I didn't feel like shooting pool with anyone, and when a hanger-on named Johnny Frank asked for a game I proposed that we get a bottle instead. He agreed and we went in search of a bottle. Actually I was only trying to kill time until Terri got off work. I planned to get her back no matter what. I was going to meet her when she got off and beg if need be; anything for another chance.

Johnny Frank and I split a fifth of Seagrams in a vacant lot, sitting in an abandoned tireless Buick. The whiskey made me sentimental, and soon I wanted to know what he thought about Terri. It didn't really matter, but still there was this itching desire to run it down to him. Only the liquor must have made me set the question up wrong, because it didn't come out cool at all.

I asked, "Dig, man. What you think about crackers?"

His look was puzzled and very clouded. "Crackers?" he finally drawled. "What you askin about crackers for? I don't think nothin about them dirty, rotten muthafuckas."

"I'm for real, man. Like, I wanna know what you really think."

"Shit," he replied.

"Spoze I told you I had me a white woman and was in love with her?"

His eyes seemed to glow with sudden anticipation as if—I don't know. I got the impression that he was about to laugh at me. "Is she rich?" he asked.

"Where the hell I'ma find a rich white woman, man?" I was now sorry that I'd even brought the subject up.

"Then you crazy," he declared. "What you want with a white gal if she ain't rich?" His face clouded over again.

"I told you, I love her," I said. "You got a woman and she ain't rich."

"She ain't white, either," he cracked, taking another pull on the bottle. After clearing his throat he asked, "What she look like?"

"She look pretty good."

"You mean she ain't pretty, right?"

"I mean she look pretty good, and she got an outasight body, too. We got a lot in common. We even go to Broadway shows together."

Suspicion spread across Johnny Frank's face again. He gripped the bottle tighter and said, "I know you crazy now. Here you is with a white woman who ain't rich and ain't pretty, and you sit here telling me that y'all got a lot in common. Who you think you talkin to, man—a fool?"

"Who *you* talkin to, muthafucka?" I was tempted to smack him, but he sensed my anger and I knew he was ready to use that bottle on me if I attacked him.

I made myself calm down. "Money and looks ain't everything. To me she ain't white, she just my woman. That's all that's necessary. I can't help it if you prejudiced."

Johnny Frank looked genuinely shocked. "*I* ain't prejudiced, them crackers is prejudiced. *They* started this color shit, not me, and they the ones who's keepin it up." He took another drink, then, after seeing I wasn't going to attack him, handed the bottle to me. I was in the process of tapping it for another swig when he asked, "Do she love you?"

I don't know why the question startled me so; I mean, it was a fair enough one. Yet I had to hold down a choke as a few drops went down the wrong pipe. I made a big thing of wiping my chin as I tried to digest the question. There was no doubt in my mind that I'd reply: "Of course she do," but I couldn't remember ever hearing her say it. I couldn't even remember having said it myself. I certainly had *felt* it; I had *thought* it. I mean, it was like sort of understood. Like, who needed to say it if it was there? Still, I couldn't help thinking that perhaps it should have been said, that the words would have made it more real. A recognized commitment less able to be broken.

Johnny Frank didn't know it, but speaking to him had been the best thing for me. I realized that love had to be spoken, and hungover as I was, I intended to speak it to Terri as soon as I possibly could. I was very anxious to leave him now. I had nothing else to say to him, especially since he was prejudiced.

I had no time for prejudiced people.

He beat me to it. "I gotta split, man," he said.

"I ain't holdin you," I responded.

I don't know why I was so angry at him, except that by his leaving first I felt that he was rejecting me, making me feel unimportant, which was exactly how I had wanted him to feel. Our eyes locked for an instant before he moved to get out of the car. I made damn sure that I was out before he was, and slammed my door to emphasize it, rocking that busted-up Buick back and forth on its tireless shocks and axles. Johnny Frank smiled, closed his door very carefully and walked away from the stripped, abandoned wreck without looking back.

I felt compelled to call out after him. "You just remember one thing. My commitment to black folks don't come through the head of my dick!"

He stopped at the door of the pool hall and looked back at me. "Mine do," he said. "That's why I like welfare."

Then he disappeared inside.

It was only a little after twelve noon, and I knew that it was nowhere near time for Terri to get off work yet, but I found myself heading toward Springfield Avenue anyway. Perhaps I could get a small glimpse of her as I passed by Jump-Off House. I needed the courage and the reassurance that seeing her once more would give me, the reassurance that I was more than an animal, the angry erotic swelling that Johnny Frank had implied I was. Johnny Frank had said "Mine do," had admitted that that's all he was—rage, sweat and lust— and maybe he was right. As far as he was concerned. If his commitment came through his dick perhaps it was because that's all he'd ever been to the world—a big black dick. That would never be my problem, it just couldn't.

As I worked my way toward Springfield Avenue I thought of the great potential love that Terri and I possessed. The day, which had started out overcast, was becoming brighter by the second. My spirits had been lifted by the alcohol, and I even found myself smiling as I anticipated seeing my sweet baby's face. The closer I got to Jump-Off House the heavier my heart beat. I didn't want to walk directly in front of the place and let her see me. I mean that would be too uncool.

When I got there, however, my plans had to change because the sun, my bosom buddy a few minutes ago, blinded me by glaring off the storefront windows so I couldn't see inside. I couldn't just stand there gawking or Terri would see me, or worse, someone would mistake me for an indecisive junkie and invite me inside to save me and give me the proper values.

I quickly walked farther on up Springfield Avenue, crossed the street, and started back down past the place. I glanced out of the corner of my eye, but every face inside was black. I turned back, stopped, looked directly inside. Still all black. Three emotions seemed to take hold of me right away—relief, which quickly descended into dismay, and finally into panic. Terri wasn't inside.

As I stood there staring through the window, I was hit by the posters and slogans against drugs. There was also a picture of Newark's black mayor with his family pasted up where passersby could view them.

Did they really think that slogans, pictures, and rhetoric against dope would stop junkies from getting high?

I made a pretense of studying pictures in the hope that Terri was merely out of the room and would return shortly. She might have gone to the toilet. I stood there so long that I became self-conscious. Where the hell was she? I couldn't stand in front of that window forever gaping at those idiotic posters and slogans. At last, I pushed open the door and went in.

I saw five desks in the place. All but one was occupied. Several addicts sat around waiting, reminding me instantly of the unemployment and welfare offices, where one sits while disinterested people silently berate one for keeping them employed and off welfare.

A tall, willowy sister sat at the desk. She had a large Afro, big hoop earrings and African-styled dress. She looked up and smiled at me.

"May I help you, brother?" she asked. Her eyes and teeth were the whitest I'd ever seen. Man! she was beautiful. I looked at her and wondered if she'd ever used dope. Her skin was very smooth and as brown as the snuff my grandmother used to dip. I found myself hoping she'd stand so I could check out the rest of her.

"I'm looking for Miss Alexander," I finally whispered.

The sister's smile didn't alter. "She's not in today. Is she your counselor?"

"I ain't no dope-fiend," I bristled. "I just wanna see her on some business." I stood there, confused and feeling threatened by this young beauty with the smile.

She didn't change her expression. "If it's important, perhaps you'd like to leave your number and I'll have her get in touch with you."

"No. No. I know where she live. I'll git in touch with her."

The sister's smile altered slightly, and a flit of curiosity crossed her face. I stood there in front of her like a naughty child, shy, embarrassed, not knowing what to do next. Outwardly our conversation was over, yet I stood there looking down into her lovely eyes and thinking that she somehow knew everything I was trying to hide from her.

Finally, she asked, "Is there anything else?"

I shook my head. I must have appeared to be some kind of nut, but I just couldn't break away from her while she sat there seeming to look into my soul, as though she knew everything. Then at last she looked down, and the spell was broken.

I turned and started for the door. Then I turned back to her. "You're beautiful," I said. "You just don't know how you—" I turned again and rushed out into the sunlight without waiting to hear if she would say anything. It occurred to me that she wouldn't have said thanks.

Outside I hopped a Public Service bus and headed toward Terri's place.

5

SHE LIVED on Prospect Street in a new high rise. It was all plush and elegant. Outside corporate VPs climbed into limos, afghans leaned against hydrants, and rich old ladies dripped diamonds and furs. Even the buildings were rich—cream-colored brick, thick thermopane windows, and luxurious terraces hanging over the sides instead of fire escapes.

Would you believe she had a doorman? The cat had white patent leather shoes, a white wool and suede uniform with gold buttons and braids, and a officer's hat.

He had everything but a saber and campaign ribbons.

For a moment I hesitated, wondering if all this righteous elegance was the reason I'd never agreed to come to her place. I didn't like the way the doorman looked over at me, or the way he half-assedly opened the door for me after asking me who I was and what I wanted. He treated me like a super-market delivery kid, not Terri's man, and I didn't exactly dig it.

Terri lived on the twentieth floor. I was amazed at the swift ear-popping uprush of the elevator; it wasn't at all like the groaning, jerking project elevators that I was used to. The long hallway on her floor even had a rug on it! Man, I couldn't help thinking that white people sure knew how to make life comfortable.

Not that I was comfortable there, or anything like that. In fact, I was damn uncomfortable. There was nothing I could connect with, no fights, roaches, junkies, no cooking smells. Nothing. I hurried down the antiseptic hallway in search of Terri's apartment.

I didn't hear anything when I pushed the buzzer, but a moment later I heard the door being unlocked. The girl who opened the door seemed mildly shocked to see me standing there. She looked so intently that I began to suspect that my fly was open or something.

She probably wished she had left her chain-lock on, I thought.

Presently she asked, "May I help you?"

"Is Terri in?" I whispered as though I were in a cancer ward or a funeral parlor.

"Oh," she exclaimed. "You must be Shadow."

"Yes," I said. Then feeling the need to explain myself, I rushed on. "I stopped by her job and they told me she hadn't been in . . ." *When was this chick going to invite me in? I* thought. That hallway was oppressing the shit out of me.

"She's not here," the girl said.

"Oh." I didn't know what to say now. I stood there wanting to run back to the comfort of my own neighborhood. But I didn't move.

"She ought to be back shortly," she said at last. "Would you like to wait for her?"

My first impulse was to answer no, but I nodded my head instead. She opened the door and I stepped inside. It was a hell of a relief to get away from those strong blue doors that faced the hallway.

"I'm Gina," she said. "Have a seat. Would you like something to drink while you wait?"

"Uh, I'll take a beer, if you got it. Kinda warm outside."

She was gone and back before I even had a chance to settle into one of the two comfortable armchairs. I allowed myself to really look her over as she handed me the beer. She had dark, wavy hair, very innocent-looking eyes above a pert nose. She was much prettier than Terri. Though short, she had a shapely body, with wide hips that made me wonder if she, too, was good in bed. My stereotypes of white women seemed to be deserting me since I'd met Terri—or perhaps I was just exchanging them since meeting her. Gina had me really wondering, and despite her air conditioning I was still hot. She sat across from me and raised her drink in a silent toast and sipped pleasurably through pursed lips as if preparing for a kiss.

"I got the impression that you and Terri were on the outs," she said.

"Well, yeah, kinda I guess. But—" I didn't know what was happening to me, but suddenly my anger rose until I had to fight it back to a level I could control. I mean, she didn't know me. What gave her the right to pry into my business? Would she have done this if I were a white man she was meeting for the first time? She was so casual about it that I wanted to put the fear of God into her. The arrogant bitch. My hand trembled and I spilled a little of the beer, and was further angered by the curious, patronizing smile on her face.

I said, "I'm hopin I can convince her that we shouldn't be on the outs." I hesitated. "Has she—I mean, do you know how she feels about it?"

Gina gave me a mysterious smile. "Terri doesn't talk much. We're really not that close, you know. I think she only told me about you—y'know, being black and all—because she thought it would shock me."

"Did it?" I asked.

She thought a moment. Then: "I don't really know if it did or not."

I didn't believe her, but I hoped my pose was intact and that she couldn't see my discomfort and my disbelief.

She kept right on talking while my thoughts drifted around her. I decided that I didn't like her even though I couldn't keep down a very real desire to feel her thighs, which she tantalized me into staring at by crossing and uncrossing her legs. I mean, they were two terrific mounds of cream.

She was saying: "I had a black boyfriend once, when I was in high school. I was sixteen. I can never remember his name. It was funny the way we never got to go to bed. He was the one who was afraid. I always thought black guys liked to do it. Not him, though, you know?"

The bitch! I kept thinking. Why couldn't she talk about something else? I couldn't keep my eyes nor my mind from wandering under the mini-skirt she wore. Every so often she would rub her own arm as she talked, and my hand longed to take her hand's place.

". . . and not once has Terri mentioned how it feels to go with a black guy—and believe me I've asked." She laughed and took a sip of her drink, which seemed to be affecting her. "We girls talk about you men as much as you talk about us, y'know."

More and more I disliked her and more and more my desire increased. "Can I have another beer?" I asked.

"You most certainly may," she replied.

I knew, as she swayed into the kitchen. I knew that she was surely inviting me—daring—to try her. She returned to find me standing and pretending to look at a picture on the wall. Gina stood by me. I took the beer and returned to my seat, momentarily losing my nerve, for I had planned to grab her and kiss her. She continued standing, looking at me over her glass with that damn smile still on her face.

I made my decision. I got up and took the few steps it required to reach her. The moment before I put my hands on her I saw a great fear replace her smile. I pulled her to me and she came without resistance. Her skin quivered under my touch, and I wasn't sure whether she welcomed me or was about to scream. When I kissed her she stood stock-still; her lips after a while became less reluctant and less uncompromising, and they opened for my tongue.

Then came her breathing, harsh, hurried. Her mouth fairly gulped my tongue. She forced her own tongue into my mouth while her arms gripped my neck like a resilient but inescapable vise. The kissing didn't last long, for she snatched her mouth away and placed it on my neck where she began to suck the skin—so much so that it hurt me.

I didn't realize what was happening at first, but soon her quivering turned into a violent shaking; her grip tightened and her body tried to merge itself with mine.

Then it hit me. She was coming in her drawers. I cursed out loud. I didn't want her to do that. I wanted to be inside of her. I tried to push her away and get her drawers down, but she wouldn't let me.

"Uhuh, uhuh, uhuh," she grunted and held me even tighter. It was over before I knew it. The spot where she had sucked my neck was throbbing with pain.

She pulled away, wide-eyed, red-faced, appearing to stare

at me and yet looking anxiously about the room as though she suspected a candid camera was witnessing her rape of me. Her hair had suddenly frizzed up. As pretty as she had been only moments before, now she looked wild and ugly. And there was a sneer on her lips.

"Get out," she said softly but firmly.

I started toward her. "Huh?"

"Get out, I said." She steadily backed away. Then louder, "Get out of here!"

I was dazed and frustrated, and suddenly very angry. My brain couldn't accept all that was happening. I mean, there was no doubt in my mind that she was rejecting me; it was so vividly etched on her face that I couldn't have missed it. But I couldn't find a reason for it. So I stood there, arms suspended in midair, dick as hard as Gibraltar, listening to this white bitch, who was responsible for it all, telling me to get out.

"If you don't leave here right now, I'm going to call the cops!" she shouted.

That did it. I took a step but she still opened her mouth and let out the loudest scream I ever remembering hearing. Immediately I turned and headed for the door.

"Nigger!" she yelled at my fast-retreating back. "Nigger, *nigger, nigger!*"

I was glad to see that plush, carpeted, chandelier-lit hallway this time. I didn't even stop to take the elevator, but took the stairs down two and three at a time all twenty floors. Once outside, I walked a long time before I allowed myself a look back over my shoulder. Each time a police car went by I nearly had a heart attack for fear that they were going to arrest me.

And, dig it, half the time I wasn't thinking of that so much as I was thinking about Terri finding out.

60

I reached for my cigarettes to calm my throbbing nerves only to discover that I'd left them behind in the apartment. It was my most sincere wish that the bitch would smoke one of them and get the worst lung cancer there ever was.

Yet I needed a smoke badly. I stopped in the first store I came to and bought a pack. I was on my way out when I saw the telephone. I dialed Terri's number.

"Hello?" Gina's voice came over the wire calm and serene.

"I won't say nothin to Terri if you don't," I said.

"I never thought you would," she replied sharply. "And if you think I'd let her know that I even let you in here, then you're even more stupid than I thought!"

She banged down the phone so hard that it hurt my ears.

6

I BOUGHT some wine on my way back home, knowing that I could always find some sort of solace inside the bottle. I didn't intend to get drunk, you dig, but I was going to juice enough to dim the pain. I mean, life was like becoming more stupid with each and every minute—and I was damned close to being wiped out by it. Without the magic bottle having the wonderful power to make ugliness go away I don't think I would have lasted much longer.

And, of course, there was Terri. I had to have her. I knew that as definitely as I knew anything, because without her everything was nothing to me.

My thoughts ran to indecision all the way back to my place. I was so tightly involved in trying to find some way out of my dilemma that I didn't even remember passing anyone I could recognize nor any of the otherwise familiar landmarks of the neighborhood. My feet were carrying me up the stairs of my building when I did finally make a decision of sorts. I would call again. That was simple.

Down the stairs I jumped and took off for the corner confectionery store before I could have a chance to change my mind. The phone stood like a desert oasis, giving me a link to Terri. There was no thought that Gina might once again answer the call. I grew braver; all she could do anyway was tell me that Terri wasn't home.

Four rings before anyone picked up the other phone and the knot in my stomach loosened when I heard Terri's voice say hello. I took a very deep breath and gripped both the receiver and my wine bottle tighter.

"Terri," I said in such a simpering tone that I got mad at myself. "It's me."

"Yes," she replied coolly.

"Can I talk to you, honey? I mean, can I see you?"

"About what?"

"About us. I have to see you, Terri. Please. I'm gon go outa my mind—you didn't work today."

"I'm helping them. Giving them a reason to fire me, if they want. I haven't been going in. What do you want to see me about? I don't think we ought to. Why not let it lie?"

"Don't you think I done tried?" I knew my voice was rising, but I couldn't control it. "What you think I been tryin to do all week long? We just gotta talk, baby. I mean, if I ever meant anything to you . . ."

There was a very long silence on her end of the line, though I could hear her breathing. Then at last she said, "You shouldn't have hit me."

I detected a weakening in her voice and my hope reached for new heights. "Honey," I blurted. "I'm sorry, I really am.

I swear 'fore God I'll never do it again. Please, baby, just let me talk to you. Just talk. I promise I won't bother you in no way." I was getting desperate, thinking that she might shine me on.

"It won't work," she said evenly. "It just won't. I can't tolerate such an act. People have minds. They can think and reason. They shouldn't need to hurt each other physically."

Something about the very even vagueness of her voice told me that I was near to winning her over. I was going to see her again. Yeah, my blow had hurt her pride, but it hadn't dimmed her desire; and then it occurred to me that I didn't know anybody who hadn't beaten their woman's behind at least once. Shit, it hadn't caused them to break up forever. I had heard that a woman needed an occasional sock in order to keep her in line, off-guard and interested. I mean, man, like didn't I know women who didn't think their men cared for them if they didn't hit them once in a while?

I suppose these thoughts emboldened me because I could feel somewhere deep within my bowels a milling around and coming together of fine, lacy pieces of my self-confidence. A new timbre heartened my voice and I nearly demanded: "You gon lemme see you, Terri? We gotta talk about this thing."

Hell, I was only half-surprised when she responded. "Alright, but I don't really see what—"

I cut right in. "I'll be at my place. You can come in about an hour, okay?"

There was the smallest bit of silence, then her breath caught and she said, "I'll be there."

"See you then, baby," I said. After hanging up the phone I zipped back home and hastily tried to straighten the dump out a bit, put it in some kind of order. Didn't help much, but my bloody red bulb was capable of hiding a hell of a lot.

The knock at my door came in a little over an hour. When

64

I opened the door I grew wobbly at the sight of her standing there so brightly dressed and freshly made-up—just for me! It was just so wonderful to see her again, dig? I grabbed her hand as if she were going to escape and led her to the sofa. I mean, like I felt so groovy, y'know?

"How ya been, baby?" I knew that my eyes were shining like new money.

"I've been fine," she answered calmly.

"I ain't," I said. "I been so fucked up since you been gone that I ain't been able to do nuthin."

"It's your own fault."

"Whatcha mean, 'my fault'?"

"If you're strong enough to beat a woman, you ought to be strong enough to be without her. I know that some women are supposed to like that sort of thing, but I'm not one of them."

Now she had a look on her face that I didn't like. I mean, it was speaking to me, telling me something I couldn't quite grasp. Like, it seemed racial, if you know what I mean. Telling me that I was inferior or something. I was animal and she was mental. I had to hold back a rising resentment inside me because it was in such direct conflict to my need of her. "I didn't beat you," I said. "I only smacked you. You won't die."

"Even so. It was unnecessary . . ."

"Look, let's forget it, huh? I'm sorry I hit you—can't you forgive me?"

She didn't say anything, just looked at me for a very long time with what appeared to be a smirk—not a smirk of ridicule, either. I mean, she seemed to be saying: *What the hell would I be doing here if you weren't forgiven?* And, gradually, I seemed to get the idea. Dig: If my hitting her was so damned repulsive to her why *would* she be here? And as my thoughts grew along these lines her look took on a less aggressive nature to me. I mean, I could detect myself growing stronger, I *felt* it, while her condescension turned submissive, if you know what I mean.

"You my woman," I stated with an even forcefulness.

"I'll have to think about that," she replied.

There was something strange going on, and I strongly sensed that I was on the verge of some great revelation. I put my hand on her arm and pulled her to me. "Ain't nuthin to think about. I said you my woman. Is you?"

She continued to stare at me and her eyes were wells of water through which I could peer all the way to the very bottom. And it seemed to me that in them, like a pretty piece of coral, was everything about her that I ever wished to know. My brain filled with a sudden, great and disastrous amount of instinctive knowledge about her. Yet in an instant the whole thing was gone, shot away from me like a satellite into orbit. It was gone leaving only a vague image of what I'd sensed and seen. I mean, dig. I knew exactly where she was at; peeped her hole-card. I really knew everything about her. I knew how she felt about me; how she would always feel about me, and that without me she would be lost to herself. She would have to feed on herself without me because, at bottom, I was her soul. She had power, but she didn't have an ounce of heart and, therefore, would always need me in a way I could never need her, except in my fucked-up imagination. She didn't have to confirm a damned thing for me. My moment of lucidity, or muddiness, passed from me as easily as it had come, and I kissed her deeply and waited for the tremors of desire that I knew would follow.

My voice quaked as I said, "Don't you ever try to be better than me again, y'hear . . ."

She placed my hand on her breast.

"Cause if you do I'ma hafta kick yo ass. I'll just hafta," I sighed.

She moved my hand down to her crotch where my fingers pushed aside her panties to touch her moist pussy. Her breath caught, her eyes rolled back and she began a sing-song moaning way down in her throat. I stood quickly and got myself undressed while she did the same at a slower pace.

Something funny was happening to me. I mean, despite my usual fascination with her white flesh—mottled here and there by marks from her clothing and other, I guess, emotional pressures—my main attraction was to her hair. I mean, like it seemed to represent something very profound and very special to me. It was good hair, if you know what I mean. There were dancing little highlights in it that made me wish it were a cool stream into which I could dive. *That's it!* I had a real urge to just wash myself in her hair; to scoop up gobs of it and wash my blackness off . . . it had the power to wash me whiter than snow.

And, by the same token, she didn't seem to be able to take her eyes or hands off my dick. Its hard curve appeared to have her enthralled much in the same manner her hair had me. Yet, and dig this, her look was not a look of mere longing. (I couldn't figure out what was making me think like this.) Hers was definitely not a look of longing; it was, if anything, one of rapacious hunger. I mean, like I could swear that she was actually drooling. And I knew right then and there that she would never be satisfied without such a dick as mine. Shit, the hope of it seemed to be what kept her alive. And I sensed with real assurance that the best thing that could have happened to her would have been to be raped by Ahmad and his gang. It would have revitalized her, given more meaning to her entire life. No white dicks could have done this for her because they held no secrets for her to uncover; nothing for which she had the slightest curiosity.

She watched closely as I moved my nakedness toward her.

She took me in hand and gently massaged her face, neck and breasts with it—as sacred an act as a ritual baptism. She, oh yes, worshiped the infinite power and reveled in the latent violence it represented, for here was a dick that could assault her. I kept thinking what a bitch she was, what a jive-ass honky bitch she was to have got me like this. Dig it! I could have killed her at that moment had it not been for my overwhelming need of her; had not my lust been so great or my will so weak.

I looked down at her, to where I was fast descending, and she opened her legs and welcomed me with a soft murmur of pleasure and relief. We moved together and I became full of the hot craving to inundate her insides with all the stored-up fluid within me. We moved. I was alternately gentle and harsh. I stroked her to the point of death, baby; to such an extent that she began so violent a trembling and became so moist that I had to strain to stay with her. Even so, I still slipped out. She quickly dried me off, then herself, and replaced me inside her. The renewed friction caused a great leap inside me. I grabbed her. For one, just one heavenly moment I felt myself about to come. Oh! It was there! At last! I worshiped the moment, and waited, hoping that it would, but not really wanting an end, no matter how much it enchanted me.

And then I felt it dying away . . . just like that it was going. Like all the other times, I was losing. I couldn't make it, had never, goddamn, made it inside her pussy. No matter how much I grunted and pushed and tried to force that muthafuckin shit out of me there was nothing, nothing but a hollow, gaseous ball left in my hollow stomach.

Terri didn't even know. She was so much into her own thing that she didn't even know . . . again. And there I was, droopy but with enough (I guess *decency* is the word, yes . . .) decency at least to wait patiently while she dug infinity by herself. My anger, of course, would be directed at both of us later on, but I also knew that I wouldn't say a damned thing. I mean, like, shit, what was there to say?:

"Er, pardon me, Terri"
"Yes."
"I can't seem to come"
"Oh, how God-awful"

Know what I mean?

After we'd had smokes and a little wine she began to fondle me. I rose immediately hard, knowing that she was going to give up some of that delicious head. To make it even better she kept some of the wine trapped inside her mouth, and when she took my johnson into it I had to catch my breath. Involuntarily I found myself raising up on my toes as the mixture of warm wine and her equally warm saliva made the head of my johnson drunk. The small slurping sounds she made increased my desire to such a great extent that I couldn't hold back the scream that began somewhere in the vicinity of my ankles and worked itself up to my constricted throat. Both of my heads opened and let out all that was trapped inside them. And when my buttocks touched back down on the bed it was as if I had just come out from under ether: there was no real memory of what had happened, only the memory of it about to happen; and the afterglow and the afterpain. The stars, circles, spirals and blackness that had sucked me under were gone.

"What's the reason?" Her question startled me and I really didn't know what she was talking about.

"What's the reason for what?" I asked through my fogged brain.

"Why can't you ever come when we make love?"

"Hell, I just came, didn't I?"

"Please don't play games. You know what I mean."

Yes, I guess I did know. I also knew that she was becoming angry. But once one begins the game with white folks—no matter how much one loves them—there's nothing to do except play it on out to the bitter end. I mean, there's never any real reason for one not to, I guess.

"Baby," I finally said. "I don't know what you talkin about."

Terri sat up in the bed. The redness on her face that had been put there by sex took on a deeper hue, bespeaking very real anger. "Goddammit!" she hissed. "You haven't once, not *once,* come inside of my cunt! Yet when I give you a blow-job you shoot off like Niagara Falls. *I want to know why.*"

I wanted to be cool. "Don't you like it?" I asked.

She took a deep breath. "Is there something wrong with you?"

I began to lose my cool. "Whachoo mean?" I replied ominously.

"Just what I said," she retorted. "Is there something wrong with you?"

Now it was my turn to sit up. "You tryin t'say I'ma freak, or somethin?"

She heaved a big sigh. "Can't we ever talk? Don't we have something, some substance to our relationship besides sex?"

"Not when you always dumpin yo shit on me," I said. "I'm a man! I'm *the man* here. You always tryin to force some shit on me—your values. Yeah, I got plenty substance, but you can't deal with it cause you too busy dealin with the fucked-up shit in yo mind."

She didn't know what I was saying, and it was obvious in the way she looked at me. It seemed as though she was trying to see straight inside my head, really trying to get it together, dig? I watched her with my heart pounding, knowing beyond comprehension that I loved this woman more than I could possibly tell. And I knew that she loved me, too. Still, there was something between us that we just couldn't overcome. I mean, it wasn't race, though there was that too, it was something a hell of a lot more than race, mere skin. It was like the rock of Gibraltar yet it was also amorphous, indescribable; it was something that was letting me in on the world's biggest secret, or joke, and at the same time it denied me any tangible means of even remotely understanding what it was about.

Terri got out of bed and began slowly dressing herself. I watched paralyzed for a long moment before I could react. Then I asked: "What's this?"

She gave me a sad look. "It's no good. I told you on the phone. It's not going to work."

I got up, stark-naked and oblivious of it. "Is you a fortune-teller, or somethin? How you know it won't work? Do you love me?" I didn't really know what I was saying, but the need to spill words, to try and stop her from leaving, was so great, and the idea of being without her again so terrible that I found tears welling in my eyes.

"Yes," she said. "I do love you."

"Well—"

"It's not enough," she interrupted. "Don't you see? It's just not enough!"

"I don't see a damn thing, except that you don't love me enough." I knew that I wasn't being either fair or truthful, but I couldn't deal with any of that; there was that thing between us. I couldn't deal with it, how was she supposed to. Yet I couldn't allow her to leave in innocence . . . not without a fight. I mean, it was her fight, too. I don't know how I got to fighting with her when all I intended to do was fight for her.

She was putting on her skirt when I grabbed her. "You

can't leave," I warned. "You my woman."

"Yes, but I'm leaving."

"No you ain't!" I raised my voice to imply a threat and felt immediately foolish, which increased my frustrated anger.

"Let me go," she said calmly. "Save both of us."

An incredibly hot rush of rage seized me. I mean, dig, the burden this cracker bitch was trying to lay on me, like I was a fucking movie hero with a white hat on. I grabbed her blouse and snatched at it until it ripped.

"I said you ain't takin a muthafuckin step!" And right away my weakness smashed my own face, and I knew that I couldn't fool either of us—not way down deep where it mattered.

She looked at her blouse, then said gently: "Will that help us?"

"Maybe not," I spat. "But this will," and I brought my hand up and across her face. She slammed down onto the bed and lay looking up at me with a blank stare. She didn't cry out as I'd expected she would, nor did she even feel the red mark I'd left on her face. I had to make myself move and I began taking her clothes off. I wouldn't look into her eyes for I didn't want to see anything that would deter me.

"Bitch," I muttered. "I'ma teach you who the man is around here, you understand? What I say goes!" I didn't expect an answer and I received none.

When she was completely nude again I stood back, momentarily confused about what to do. I mean, my actions seemed so meaningless. I tore her clothes off when all I had to do was ask her to take them off and she probably would have done it. She lay there, calm, very serene, looking at me and waiting for my move since it was my game. I looked at her body. I couldn't even raise a hard. I saw that delicious white body waiting for me to do whatever I wanted to it but

I couldn't raise a hard. I had to come into that pussy. That was the only way I could save us. If I could do that then everything would be alright; it would all work out. I put my hand on my johnson and tried to stimulate it. I wanted my dick to leap up and beat her down; to drown her insides with blazing semen so that she'd never again dare to humiliate me.

Nothing.

Nothing.

Not a damn thing.

I stood there holding myself in hand; sweat from my emotional turmoil gathering to soak my body. I looked into Terri's eyes, she turned her head away, and I felt so feeble, so wan and puny. I was about to give up and fall to my knees in front of her, just declare myself to be every vile, jive piece of shit she and every other white person ever thought a black man was. But from somewhere within me a picture, another force was generating itself. I clearly saw the sister who worked at Jump-Off House. She loomed up and smothered my senses. Her black beauty enveloped itself around Terri. I mean, it was as though Terri's white skin was being peeled off and the sister's was replacing it in the smooth strokes of some unknown master artist.

I watched, fascinated, awestruck, and growing harder by the second. I closed my eyes and saw the sister's beauty come alive for me. She reached her arms out to me and took my hands. When I opened my eyes my hands were touching Terri. I felt no shock at such a strange metamorphosis. It all seemed so natural to me. I felt deep rhythms in my blood as it coursed its way through my body and centered around my temples, my throat and my groin. The vibrations were steady as I looked at Terri's creamy thighs. I felt not a single contradiction in all this; and the thighs yielded like luscious marshmallows to my desperate touch.

She was moaning again, happy and hopeful that this would be her time of worth; that she would receive her woman's due. And soon again, as I watched her face contort and her hair get limp and sticky, I became as limber as a wet paper towel. The entire image of my illusioned desire dissipated. I raised up slowly, looking at her and trying to determine her thoughts. But she kept her eyes closed and her face averted. She had come again and she probably needed time to feel at least a measure of her success before trying to deal with the failure that I constituted for her.

I finally rolled away from her and lay on my back feeling a chill that was as much from her as it was from the sweat drying on my body.

"Don't say nuthin," I warned.

She kept her eyes closed. "I didn't intend to," she said.

WAP! I let her have a backhand slap. "I said don't say nuthin!" I yelled. "I mean *don't say nuthin—*nuthin at *all!*"

My breathing was more harsh than even hers. I sounded like an asthmatic. I had to find some way to beat her, even if it was only temporary. I had to make her crumble, and the only way I could do that was to come inside her body. Not, mind you, that I had anything to prove to me. I had come in a lot of women. But I had to prove it to her. I mean, it was the only thing she would accept. Maybe it was so strange because it was so real.

"I know what you thinkin, Terri," I said. "But you better not breathe a word of it out loud. You thinkin I ain't a real man, ain't you? You thinkin I'm just like them white boys you been runnin from, huh? Well, I ain't! I'm me, y'hear? I'm proud and I'm black, you hear me? I could satisfy you all night. I'm strong and I'm proud of me, you hear . . . ?"

She turned over and looked at me, not hostile or anything like that; she just looked. It was as if she could see me but not hear me. It wasn't even like listening to someone talking to you in a language you don't understand. Instead it was a look that saw all there was to see, but without caring to comprehend a fucking thing.

I became so full of my own futility that I couldn't hold myself in check any longer. I didn't try to hold back either my tears or the scream I let out as I flipped her over onto her stomach. I concentrated all my energies on her big behind then, and by sheer, torturing willpower I managed to make— and I mean *make*—my johnson rise. I think it was the only time in my life that I was able to exercise complete control over it. It rose—not with a natural sexual accumulation, but rather with a vengeful determination. No sex-hard, this. It was a hard that was unfeeling, uncaring; wild, chaotic destroyer.

I descended on her behind. I gripped her buttocks tightly and watched them become two mounds of dimples. And then I plunged in, anticipating and gleefully grunting at her yelp of pain. I felt nothing for her at the moment and I near tore her asunder. She bit her lip until it bled; her arms flailed about and she tried to throw me off by attempting to buck and turn over. But I held her. She was no match for my near-insane grip. I held her face down in the pillow until she almost suffocated, and when she was nearly out I pushed my johnson farther inside.

I could hear myself repeating: "Stinkin bitch! Honky whore!" because I couldn't get it all in and that fueled my rage.

Suddenly I jerked myself up and spread her buttocks as far apart as I could get them. Then I yakked up a big wad of spit and let it go with all the force I could muster. It landed on target, right in the middle of her little brownish hole. It must have had some kind of cooling effect after the burning of my too-large johnson because she sighed with visible relief. Then I worked her buttocks together, spreading the saliva like hot butter on bread. Strangely enough I felt a warming sensation begin to churn up inside me; I felt good and powerful, as arrogant as a New York cabdriver.

Once again I plunged, and this time her body's resistance was much less. I only had to stroke a few times before I was completely swallowed up by her. She gulped me down like a dog ripping off a mouthful of fat meat. I was sure that I even heard her let out a moan of pleasure mixed in with surprise, though it may only have been the sudden weight of my body causing her to expire some of the tension inside of her.

I stroked with one purpose: to shoot off inside her. And moments before I did I was shocked myself to find that she was socking it back to me. I mean, she was really getting down; the bitch was enjoying it, getting some mean rocks. That made me mad. I mean, dig it: here I was trying like hell to prove a point, trying my damnedest to get over a mental hump by humiliating her and the jive bitch was digging on it like a fucking masochist. My anger raced with my sexual desire to the explosive finish, and the desire only won out a second before the anger was about to erupt. I pulled myself out of her and gave her a vicious whack on her ass.

"There, bitch!" I wheezed. "You got some good black come in you now. Satisfied?"

She turned on her side and looked at me. "I'd rather have it in my cunt where it belongs."

"Why?" I asked.

"Because I've never had it there. I feel dry and empty inside. My own come isn't enough to sustain me. Can't you understand that?"

"Fuck you," I said.

"You mean half-fuck me, don't you?" she shot back.

"You better go get that cloth and wipe my dick off."

As she went into the bathroom I tried to figure out what was the matter with me. I mean, what the hell did she really want, and how could I make her see that it wasn't just my problem? She surely shared an equal amount of guilt because I was more than positive that I had enough love in me to give. She wanted my very essence; she demanded my soul, and I was unable to give her that. I mean, there aren't really any blue-eyed soul-folks, are there?

She had my heart, it was impossible to give her everything, for there were places in my mind that even I didn't know existed; where little light—and no white—entered. Places long ago set aside and established as forbidden to friend and foe alike, until something higher and mightier than myself opened up the floodgates that were capable of releasing something in me that could change the world—blasting out of each dimension a dimension of its own . . . brand-new perhaps, and complete.

But until then what could I do? Where was our place in all of this bullshit, and what, indeed, was our function? Can you dig it?

Terri returned from the bathroom and wiped me clean with the warm, soapy cloth. I noticed that she didn't look at me, not even a stolen glance, and she was oppressively silent. So much so that I finally just had to ask: "So what the fuck's the matter with you now?"

"Nothing," she replied.

"Tell me somethin better than that," I demanded.

Now she looked at me. "What's the use!" she said as she flung the soiled cloth to the floor. She raised her fists above her head. "What the hell's the use! You don't—and never could—understand. Not in one million years. God! what have I got myself into!"

I raised up. "What'd you come down here for? Who sent for you, bitch?"

"I thought there was hope—I wanted to help . . ." she trailed off.

"Help who? Ain't y'all got dope-fiends in the suburbs? You ain't interested in no black junkies. Shit! You came down here for one reason: cause ain't life in you. Ain't no real life in them goddamn suburbs, with yo fuckin crabgrass cocktail parties. You gotta come here t'suck blood back into yo white ass, cause without black folks you ain't even got a reason to live!" I was completely out of bed now and my finger was stabbing her in the face like a fencing foil.

"You're a liar!" she shouted back at me; her hands were covering her ears as if to shut out what I said. "Liar, liar!"

I'd had enough. I mean, I hadn't had enough of her, but I couldn't deal with her on this level. It was like fighting an army of ghosts, a losing battle with myself, like really trying to punch out my own shadow.

She was near hysteria and I was near to making a punk out of myself over her by taking her in my arms and trying in some stupid way to smooth everything over. How the hell can you do that after you've indicted, tried and sentenced her whole race? I could only do what I didn't want to do.

"Put yo fuckin clothes on and git out. Git the hell outa here," I said.

Her incredulity made her calm return. I'm sure you couldn't have ever made me see that I'd be saying something as drastic as that to her. I mean, man, an hour ago I had been begging her to be with me. And she certainly couldn't have known that I was merely speaking out of my deep sense of frustration. But the point is that I couldn't have made myself take it back either. Nobody gets reparations in this world.

And in the silence that followed my demand I knew that

we both were waiting for me to take it back. God knows, I wanted to. But there are just certain things a man can't do with a woman, especially not with a white woman. Dig it, she's already condescended and she'll have to kill, if you demand an encore.

Well, after dressing herself, Terri headed for the door. She didn't look back until she had reached it. Then she looked back, not at me but at the room. It was a lingering gaze, as if she was leaving something very dear, with sorrow, or something very horrible, with relief. I couldn't tell which. Her last look was at the crumpled sofa bed. Then she closed the door softly behind her and I heard her footsteps going easily down the steps.

The wine was on the table; I grabbed it and turned it up, taking large, greedy chugs until I almost choked myself. I sat on the floor and drank it all down, feeling the warmth of it flow throughout my body, knowing that it was a prelude to a heavy drunk, and not giving a damn. I lay down then and stared up at my red bulb. It made no difference if the haze surrounding it was filled with the holocaustic screamings of death. I could smile at death. I saw Ahmad's face and before I closed my eyes I winked at it.

7

WHEN ONE is on foreign turf feeling lost, alone and unwanted, there's only one thing to do: return to your own. I don't know whether I made the decision consciously, but the very next day I hurried to the Nyumba Ya Ujamaa African Shop and bought myself three dashikis, a pair of jump boots, a package of incense and *The Autobiography of Malcolm X*. It was like going for a course in "How to Be Black in One Easy Lesson," but I felt a very real need to reject Terri and everything else that was white.

It sounds ridiculous, but then a lot of people got instantly black in recent years, and there was no reason I couldn't be saved in the same manner. And I also resolved to find the biggest, blackest, thickest-lipped woman I could; I was bound and determined to love her as if she were the complete soul of all things black and African. I even thought about learning Swahili, till it occurred to me that there wasn't one person I knew who'd understand a word I'd say.

My dilemma wasn't vocal anyway. I knew black talk as well as any nigger on the street. No, I had to deal with my head. At that moment I was bulging with messianic fervor, for I was going to find a negro woman (small *n*) and make her into a black woman-weapon that would help destroy my enemies in the white race.

And so weeks passed without me seeing Terri; and though she was never out of my thoughts for long I succeeded in becoming involved with a number of black women—ugly as hell, all of them—some whom I'd known before and others who were as new as my resolve. With all of them I was near bursting with first heats of passion. And I had no trouble coming inside those who allowed me to cop. One thing, though: For the life of me I couldn't sustain the emotion. It was hot sperm, cold spawn, if you know what I mean. And, oh good Lord, I found out that some of our Black Revolutionary Queens were as frigid and as fucked up as white women were supposed to be, as far as dealing with sex was concerned.

One chick named Sylvia outdid the sexual innocence of Doris Day, while another, Barbara, hunted for the material security that might do honor to one of the Gabor sisters. But the one who really got my bowels in an uproar was the cute little broad with the round black eyes and the sweet black soul—good old Sweet Sue. The bitch was in love with Jesus —and I don't mean a Puerto Rican either. This dude, two-thousand years dead already, was giving some stiff competition. She wanted me but, dig this, she couldn't get his finger out of her pussy long enough for me to get my dick in. I persevered to the end, however, because I know that no amount of spiritual fucking can beat the real thing. It was an extra nut for me when, with the full measure of my throbbing meat swelling her insides, I'd make her deny him ten-times thrice. I'd have her in a groovy buck, then I'd say: "Who you love more, me or Jesus?"

"Oh, you! Lordy, yes, you!!!"

"Who yo God, me or Jesus?"

"Ssssssh, you is, honey. Oooooh! You is!"

Yeah, I know where it's at, when you get down to the nitty-gritty. But after the first time in bed she kept talking about getting married. I didn't want to hear that.

Besides, she really couldn't screw worth a damn.

Am I a male chauvinist pig? If I am why have so many women been able to control my life? All the things that ever mattered to me seemed to have been in their hands. The only thing in my hands is my hard dick . . . and judging by my experiences with Terri even that's in doubt. But I'm not going to dwell here on my involvement with other women, even though it tempts the hell out of me to do so.

Suffice it to say that during the time of my separation from Terri I didn't lack for pussy and a good rock-busting time.

I did, though, become increasingly angry at Terri, and, because of her, at white people in general. I was now militant. Like, the idea of seeing her get raped by Mojo, Ahmad, Cootie and Sam took on gratifying appeal for me. In fact, I guess the thought so fascinated me that I toyed with the idea of approaching them about it. Now I don't really know if I would have done it just then, but I do know that I must have had something in mind because I began hanging around the particular joints that I knew they frequented. I lost some of the fear I'd had about being in their presence, and the lost fear must have had to do with vengeance.

I knew, for instance, that the gang would nearly always be at Spoon's Bar after 11:00 P.M. and I began going there every night. They picked at me something awful at first, but I wasn't slack in defending myself against their barbs and boasts. And they didn't doubt that I'd come to blows with one or all of them if need be. I was nobody's punk. Punks can't survive in anybody's ghetto, man. You either "git down or git out," understand? So we merely traded insults instead of steel or lead.

Until one Friday night at Spoon's when Sam got very drunk and decided to really try me.

"Look, man," I said. "I ain't here to fight you."

"I was *born* to fight crackas and *neegroes* like you," he snapped back. "You ain't shit!"

I didn't reply, but I sat easy and loose on the bar stool. Then he came to me like some dude in a western movie and deliberately knocked my drink out of my hand.

Spoon, who always kept a wary eye on us, said, "Sam, that ain't cool, man. I can't afford to have no shit in my place. The A.B.C. board is already on my ass."

Sam sneered. "The muthafucka can always come outside— if he ain't a scared punk."

"Why?" I said. "So y'all can jump me?"

Cootie spoke up. "Aw, man, ain't nobody gon jump in. Ain't that right, Mojo?"

"That's right," Mojo answered. "Nobody in the world."

I looked around the bar and saw that everyone in the place was waiting for me to take the challenge so they could see a fight, or take low so they could have a good laugh. Either way it would be a significant part of the night's diversion and entertainment. Dig this: Not one person in the joint spoke out in favor of black folks being peaceful and respectful toward each other. No black unity or nationalism here except in misery.

And as I looked over the faceless faces surrounding me I

felt cursed with a deepening despair; cursed by the old crabs-in-a-basket theory, which all of my life people had assured me was true and generic to negroes. No help. No help anywhere. They weren't the people I'd recognized and greeted when I'd first entered, and desperation crept over me. The only injustice they recognized was their own personal injustices. *"Look What They Done to My Song, Momma,"* a voice wailed from the jukebox; and fleetingly I wondered what had been done to all of us.

These people, *my so-called people,* were trying to deny my existence. And at this moment I was so aware that they were me and I them. *I was them!* I had sandals, beads and an Afro to prove it.

Finally, when my eyes focused, Sam was standing over me.

"I won't fight you unless I have to, Sam," and I had to fight back a strong desire to add: *"I ain't afraid either."*

"You hafta," he retorted.

Still no one spoke. I waited out their silence, then got up. "Awright, brotha, let's git it on then."

He sneered, "You ain't non'a my brotha, nigga!"

Suddenly I was outside in the cool night air with driving fists, grunted curses, blood, sweat and the stink of alcohol stifling me. I was swinging wildly, and the screams of the crowd filled my head with mad sounds. I couldn't even see straight. At times I saw four Sams; my desperation grew and I knew beyond a doubt that I was fighting for my very life, as fearfully real as if I were wading through rice paddies in Nam with a million Vietnamese charging in righteous indignation at me. I remember my own screams drowning out those of the crowd, and my body going out of my control, possessed by some unknowable survival spirit which only the very worst disaster could overcome, and the very worst it could be was my death.

It was no longer Sam in front of me.

I battled every embarrassment and every frustration I'd ever suffered. It became every white person/cop in the world. It was Lester Maddox and his axehandles; it was Bull Conners and his dogs; it was William Buckley and his highbrowed mealymouthed justifications. And I was in the middle, screaming and hitting and tearing and hitting. Hitting. I saw the brightest colors I'd ever looked at in my life. It was everything and nothing, and I was alone.

Hands were gripping my arms and snatching at my neck, and when I came to myself I saw that my own hands had ripped Sam's mouth open. I had torn it almost to his ear.

"Shadow!" some unrecognizable voice was yelling at me. "Goddamn, man, that's enough!"

A woman's voice cried hysterically, "Don't let him kill him!" over and over again. "Don't let him kill him!"

But I did want to kill. Not just Sam. I wanted to kill anything and everything. *He must die!* my mind kept blasting the back chambers deep inside my head. *He must die so I can live!* And I felt it strange that now, when I seemed to be doing exactly what their previous silence had forced upon me, they disapproved.

Then I was standing on shaking legs, unable to recall how I got there or why my clothes were in shreds, or what Sam was doing lying in a pool of blood, snorting like a slaughterhouse pig and giving out with the widest, toothiest grin I'd ever seen. My hands felt wet and sticky. I looked and saw them covered with blood. The reality of what had occurred, slowly, by degrees, drifted back to me.

"I wanna wash my hands," I murmured softly to no one in particular. One of the men led me back into Spoon's and to the rest room, talking all the while though I could not seem to make sense of anything he said.

85

When I came out of the rest room, after the shock of cold water had somewhat cleared my head, I was hit by another, even greater, shock. The jukebox was blasting out a loud Charles Earland tune and the fingerpopping, hip-twitching good times were rolling along as if nothing had happened at all.

Not everyone was so involved that they had forgotten me. Despite the hot pursuit of moist pussy and big dick, some were aware that near murder had taken place. They had been touched in some small way by the havoc that I'd wreaked and they'd viewed.

And there were the admirers, too.

I didn't speak to anyone; I don't think I could have said anything anyway. I didn't even wave goodbye to Spoon, though he did acknowledge my leavetaking by pressing a pint of Seagrams into my hand. I'd completely forgotten about Mojo, Cootie, Ahmad and, to a degree, Sam. In any event, none of them were still around. I remember someone saying that they'd taken Sam to the hospital.

8

I HAD a sleepy, dreamless night, akin to that first night after I'd met Terri. It was only the hard, insistent knocking at my door that woke me up. The light coming in through my dingy window told me it was morning.

I came fully awake, thinking and fearful that Sam might have died and the police were here to take me away. But I soon realized that this was no police knock, though it seemed just as demanding. I didn't know how stiff and sore I was until I tried to get up, then the little creaks and pains spoke to me as if they resented the strain I'd placed upon them last night. I opened the door without even asking who it was and received a jolt of pure oxygen when I saw Mojo, Ahmad and Cootie standing outside in their full regalia of Levi's, political buttons, military patches and dark glasses. Immediately I was scrambling in my small closet for my near rusty .25 automatic, and before they stepped inside I had it in my hand.

"Hold it, man!" Mojo called out. "We ain't here to fuck with you. We just wanna rap."

I stood facing them, shaking because of my nerves, but not out of any sense of fear. I stood buck naked with my gun in my hand. "About what?" I asked.

"Kin we come in and sit?" he asked politely.

"Come ahead." I waved them in, making damn sure I kept a safe distance between us. Ahmad was clutching a brown paper bag, which he attempted to hand to me. After seeing my gun hand flinch, however, he smiled nervously, reached inside, and brought out a quart of Schenley's.

"Ain't no Molotov, baby. It ain't nuthin but plain alcohol." He opened it, took a heavy swig and then handed it to Cootie.

"What y'all wanna rap about?" I asked again.

"You," Mojo said, "and us."

"I'm listenin. Speak on it."

Cootie passed the bottle to me.

"Dig, brotha," Mojo began. "We been rappin bout you since last night. I mean, we dug the real you. And so we figgered we mighta been too hard on you in the past. It don't do to mess over a brotha who can deal like you can, see?"

"Whatchoo gittin at, man?" I demanded. The whiskey hit the spot. I was growing bolder by the minute, so much so, that I even put the gun down long enough to slide into my pants.

"I'm gittin at the fact that we black folks got too many enemies in the white race already, so we shouldn't be tryin to off each other."

"That's right!" Cootie put in. "Imperialist crackas and bourgeois niggas is our real enemies. Foes of the oppressed."

Mojo snapped at him. "Let me do the talkin, man!"

A tense, challenging look passed between them for a moment; but Cootie dropped his eyes first, so Mojo continued: "Brotha, when you was fightin Sam last night you was the epitome of what the Third World revolutionary man oughta be. I mean, you was the pure fightin machine: quick and deadly. Askin no quarter and sho-nuff not givin none. You was the kind of man that brotha Malcolm X and brotha Eldridge Cleaver would be proud of. And even though Sam is our comrade, we could appreciate the fact that you's our comrade, too."

I had to smile. "Y'all like me now, huh?"

Ahmad stood. "That ain't got nuthin t'do with it," he said. "A comrade is a comrade whether ya like 'im or not. We got the same capitalist foot in our ass as you got. That's enough t'make us see where we at and what we oughta be dealin with, if we don't wanna git wiped out."

My mind jumped directly to Terri; if not because she was an enemy, then surely because of her whiteness. She was at least a growing symbol of my hatred and self-loathing. She fed my social and sexual frustrations. White folks rejected black folks, and she had rejected me.

I wanted to bring her up, since she represented so much of their resentment toward me. "Y'all don't care about me messin with . . ." I trailed off. It seemed too personal, none of their business; yet I wanted them to say something.

"If you mean yo white woman, man, forgit it," Mojo said with a voice full of understanding. "Where you put yo dick is yo business."

"She ain't my woman no more. We broke up." I went to the closet and pulled out my new dashikis. "This is where I'm at from now on. The only thing white I want is my eyes and my teeth."

They all laughed with me, but then Mojo, urged on by

Cootie, who seemed to be getting uneasy, said, "Dig, man. This business we came to see you about . . ."

"Yeah?"

"Well, we'd like to know if you wanna hook up with us. Y'know that fight last night really shot yo stock up in this community. People talkin bout you all over the place."

The others nodded in agreement. Mojo rushed on: "But all they gon do is talk. You ain't gon git a damn thing, cept maybe a few pats on the back, then they gon soon forgit. Know what I mean?"

I merely nodded my head and continued listening.

"Now you can be a bad dude in this community if you wanna be," he predicted. "And you can try livin off yo rep and tell us t'go fuck ourselves. But we think it'd be hipper for you to join up with us so that we can begin to deal with some of the cold shit goin down around here."

I took the last of their whiskey and drained it. "I still don't see where y'all comin from, man . . ."

Mojo took a deep breath and eased it out slowly. He surveyed the cracked, sagging ceiling, the red overhead bulb, and said, "I mean that you ain't properly politicized, man. This gon be an all-black city after while and we oughta be together so we can have some real Black Power. Dig: business is movin out, crackas movin out with the money, and City Hall is tearin down buildins and ain't puttin a damn thing up that we can use. We don't see no black group mobilizin to fill the gap, cause they's either too black or too negro to mobilize the people. And no matter what ideals they got ain't none of em feedin the people; poverty pimps or Ford Foundation-approved revolutionaries is what they is. So we believe that we got the nucleus of a real revolutionary force that can do alla us some good—"

"You gon feed the people?" I asked almost laughing out loud.

Mojo fixed me with a hard, level stare. A hint of a sneer pulled his lips back against his teeth and he said coldly: "We can make them think so, if we play it right. And, in any case, we won't do no worse than anybody else is doin—"

"Man," Cootie spoke up, "we can control this whole mutha-fuckin city in two years!"

I couldn't control my laughter this time. "You is dreamin, nigga."

"Is this nightmare we in any better?" Cootie was on his feet pointing his finger in my face and waving his other hand at my sordid, poverty-row surroundings—the frayed, torn furniture, the broken plaster, the bare sweating pipes, all of it shimmering in the red glow of the bulb. He then let it out with a high-pitched snarl that grated my raw, jumping nerves like heavy-duty sandpaper.

"Shit!" he yelled. "We ain't talkin bout savin the whole fuckin world, man. We ain't dumb enough t'think we gon really control things. We ain't even got no capital. We ain't got no land and we don't produce a goddamn thing we could market. We ain't got the airport, seaport, railway or the fuckin highway. But we know that we could be the middle-man; we know we could be the center that all this shit revolves around. The Jews did it, and they finally bought themselves a country to go to if things ain't right here. We could do the same thing startin right here. The idea would touch every nigga in this country who ever wanted to walk down some street somewhere and not be burdened by the fuckin color of his skin."

Cootie sat down, his face gleaming with sweat, not so much from his emotional exertion as from the fact that he needed a fix. This was great.

How can you conduct a revolution when you're high?

The realization of his condition had suddenly dulled the fires of revolution that had burned brilliantly and briefly in his eyes, so I addressed myself to Mojo and Ahmad because Cootie no longer even looked interested in continuing the conversation.

"All that sounds good," I said. "But I still think y'all dreamin . . ."

"About what?" Ahmad asked.

"About runnin the town," I replied.

Mojo said, "Fuck the town for now, man. Let's deal with runnin our community, our own street. Let's talk about controllin the space where we at. We don't wanna git wiped out and we don't wanna take on more than we can handle, but if we gon ever git over the hump we gon hafta start somewhere.

They sat looking at me, waiting for a reply that I was in no way prepared to give them. I wanted to, mind you. Despite the fact that I knew where they were at, that I knew them for the rip-off artists, strong-arm punks and muscle bums they were, part of me was still for them, wanted me to accept. These guys made me feel damn good, if you can dig it. I could almost forget our entire past relationship. I mean, these cats had a *need* for me.

"Looka here," I said at last. "Y'all gimme some time to think about this. I don't mean about us bein friends and brothas—"

Cootie snapped to: "Ain't nobody my brotha who ain't my comrade first!" And again there was his finger, with its dirt-caked nail, stabbing at my face, the voice high-pitched with emotion. "We don't need brothas who ain't willin t'be comrades. We be glad as hell to have you with us, y'understand. But you ain't gon stop us by blowin us away right now. Even as we talkin right now there's other dedicated people mobilizin. You can't stop the revolution."

"I know the way you guys feel," I said. "And I know that beatin one of you or even killin one of you ain't beatin or killin all of y'all. But right now I got problems, personal problems. My head's fucked up and I gotta git it together before I make any definite moves . . ."

"I can understand that," Ahmad sympathized.

Mojo added: "Yeah. Me too. But how long before you let us know where you at?"

"Gimme a week to think about it. I need at least a week."

The two of them looked at each other. Cootie had his eyes closed.

"Right on, brotha," Mojo said, rising from his seat. "You got it." He extended his hand and one by one I gave them the nationalist handshake: first the traditional grip, then locking thumbs, back to the traditional, then locking fingers and finally placing balled fists over our hearts. I'd always considered it a time-consuming action, but some dudes got real uptight if the decorum wasn't strictly adhered to. Some even judged your degree of blackness by it, so it was always safer to go all the way with it.

I walked them to the door. As he passed me Cootie said, "We goin t'see Sam at the hospital." He made it seem as though I was supposed to send a get-well card or something.

"Tell him I said 'Hi'." I closed the door in his face.

9

Now I had one hell of a question to answer. I mean, dig. I knew for a fact that I loved Terri. And I also knew that despite what the gang did or how they acted, they believed in black unity. But I was confused. I mean why did the two loves have to cancel each other out? Why couldn't I have both?

At least Mojo and the gang needed me, if only because I had displayed to them the awesome fact of my violence. To them I was a bad muthafucka! Yeah. Shadow the Terrible—big with his fists, big with his mouth.

And what was I to Terri? A big black dick, only one that couldn't come.

In the end, I decided to join the gang. My life at present was meaningless, and they at least had a purpose. I wasn't helping Terri any, and I sure as shit wasn't helping myself. I could be of use to no one if not black people, or rather, to a hazy concept of what black people were supposed to be. I knew that I was no Malcolm X or Martin Luther King, and I would probably never inspire anyone on a national scale, but following Booker T. Washington's advice, I was going to throw down my goddamn bucket where I was. Deal with people on their level.

I knew I'd find my troops at Spoon's so that's where I headed as darkness covered the city and turned Newark into a vast network of ill-lit streets, a welter of honking cars, thousands of dark, cheap dives where black Newarkers found surcease from daily toil.

As I made my way downtown I was impressed by the great amount of traffic heading up and out of town. This was another daily occurrence, as the white folks began their escape to the suburbs in locked cars, stealing glances at the black natives whom they passed, and angered at the traffic jams they themselves caused in their haste to flee the city. They made Broad, Market, West Market streets as well as Springfield and South Orange avenues endless chains of cars from 3:30 P.M. to 6:30 P.M., and many were the black folks who gathered on these streets just to watch and laugh at the honky's daily discomfort.

It seemed one way to get even and to temporarily forget a deeper pain.

When I finally did reach Spoon's, Mojo, Ahmad and Cootie were seated at the bar talking revolution, drinking beer and trying to hustle three women who appeared to spend every waking hour in the joint. Don't get me wrong, these chicks weren't prostitutes, they lived in the area, which was mostly housing projects and factories. They were such frequent inhabitants of Spoon's because it was *their* fun. The whiskey was cheap, the music was loud and they were at home. I mean, contrary to what many white people think, blacks don't feel comfortable with all blacks. For the denizens of Spoon's to go, for instance, to a club that had some semblance of elegance and sophistication, such as Mr. Wes', The Playbill, or Mr. C's, was close to and often equal to dining at Sardi's and catching the show at The Copacabana afterward. Spoon's was a neighborhood bar, and those who worked hard at their jobs worked just as hard at their fun in Spoon's. That most of the men had been to bed with most of the women was due to their close proximity rather than to their inclination. I mean, dig it, even a rock wears down if you rub it long enough. You don't even have to rub it hard. Only occasionally would a fight break out over someone being caught with someone else's stuff, but after it was over things went quickly back to normal.

I walked over to my troops. It was amazing the way they seemed to snap to at my approach. Man, I felt fabulous! I guess that's the way a movie star feels. And right away I began to feel that I hadn't made a bad decision. I knew what it felt like to really be needed.

As cool as I could I said, "I done made up my mind."

"Is you with us?" Mojo inquired.

"No!" I snapped back. "I ain't with y'all—I'm leadin y'all."

Ahmad jumped up and slapped my palm. "Right on, baby!"

I noticed that Cootie hadn't seemed to like the way I had approached them. He acted preoccupied with the babe seated next to him.

"You don't seem too keen about it, Cootie," I said.

Mojo jumped in. "Oh, he just high, man. He ain't too keen on a damn thing right now except gittin higher and gittin some hot guts from that bitch he talkin to."

The girl, a short, light brown broad named Agnes, flushed

dark with indignation. "Don't call *me* no bitch, you black-ass muthafucka! Yo *mammy*'s a bitch!"

Mojo didn't get angry. He smiled and said, "I didn't call you no bitch, whore, I said *'that* bitch.' Is you necessarily *that* bitch?"

Agnes became confused. Her mouth opened, but nothing came out, and her silence bespoke the fact that she couldn't find a way around his sophistry. However, she intended to have the last word.

"Spoon!" she called out. "Give me, Cootie, Ahmad and Shadow a drink, please."

Not having heard their exchange, and never one to miss a sale, Spoon said, "Ain't Mojo in the party, baby?"

Agnes smiled as she enjoyed her true vindication. Daintily she retorted, "I ordered for the parties whom I ordered for, *Mister* Spoon."

Mojo was about to become angry, but I broke in fast. I mean, after all, this was my moment, and I wasn't about to lose it to some bitch over a couple of cheap drinks.

"One thing I want straight," I said, "before y'all start hittin that juice."

"What you want straight?" Cootie brayed back harshly.

I looked him dead in the eye. "If I'm *playin,* I'm *sayin.* There ain't gon be but one leader."

The bitch tried to bring attention back to the drinks Spoon was serving up, but I shot her a look, and her gaping mouth sucked up the words before she could say them.

No one else responded. I went on. "Like you cats know more revolutionary rhetoric than me, but I know how to supply the troops. And that makes me special. So from now on if I don't think somethin is right you guys gon hafta listen even if there's a chance I'm wrong. That's what a leader's for. Y'all got that?"

I looked at them each in turn and waited as each nodded his agreement. If any of them dissented it didn't show. I was not only a revolutionary now with the jump boots and dashikis to prove it, I was also the commanding general of the nation's newest liberation army.

I'd come a long way from the factory and had a distance yet to go.

10

I KNEW that my leadership role would be doomed in short order unless I provided my troops with action and supplies, and I had to do it fast, too. My instincts told me that much. And even if they hadn't, Cootie was always there to run off at the mouth:

"When we gon *move*, man?" he'd complain. "Shit, we did more than this before you became leader . . . and ahm tireda sittin around teachin you bout revolution. You can't *talk* revolution, you gotta *make* revolution. I say we need to *move!*"

He always seemed to care more about the revolution when he needed a fix. At these times liberating the enemy's cash supplies seemed to be of paramount importance, and by now his revolutionary zeal was at an all-time high.

We were sitting in my pad after one of their visits to Sam at the hospital, when Cootie again started his usual lament about our inactivity, and more specifically our lack of legal tender.

"Don't worry," I said, "I got somethin planned that in a few days'll have our names ringin all over this town. Then," I gave Cootie a menacing look, "we gon see how ready you is for action and for revolution, brotha Cootie."

"I'm always ready," he shot back. "How long *you* been in the game, anyway?"

"How long ain't important. It's how many points you score. Can you dig it?"

I didn't feel like pacifying Cootie anymore so I changed the subject. More out of desperation than concern I said, "I'll tell y'all about it in a few days. How's Sam doin?"

"He alright," Mojo replied. "Only gotta be there for another week; then he be ready to come home for good. But he gon have a helluva scar unless he git money for plastic surgery."

"Y'all tell'im about me?" I asked.

"Yeah."

"Well . . . ?"

"Well, what?"

"Well, what the fuck did he say!" I half-shouted.

Mojo seemed genuinely surprised at my outburst. "What can he say after," he said, pointing to himself and the others, "we done voted you in. He know the way things go. He either with us or against us, and if he against us then he out."

"I'm goin with y'all tomorrow to see him," I said impulsively.

Ahmad asked with a sly smile, "You think he ready for that?" It was a sincere query.

"Whether he is or not," I replied, "he gon have to deal with it."

Sheer bravado inspired the next idea. It was bold, but Cootie was right. It was time for action, and I felt up to anything at the moment. The North-Central Pool Hall on the fringe of the Italian neighborhood in Newark's North Ward was the scene of an uneasy truce between black and white. Toleration rather than friendship existed there, with the Puerto Ricans quickly learning that in spite of their lighter skin and straighter hair, they too were niggers. All the races went there because it had the best tables in town and more money flowed for betting. This was where I planned to unveil the Revolutionary Vanguard of the People of Newark.

"Jus watch," I said grinning, "tonight we got business at the North-Central Pool Hall." Mild surprise showed on Cootie's face. "You wanted action. You wanted the revolution to move, well this is yo chance to put it in gear, baby."

Time passed quickly as we sat around juicing and bullshitting, and before anyone realized it evening had come. We were feeling good, but more important than that we felt bold.

No one hesitated when I finally announced: "It's time to move, y'all."

We walked through the street two abreast, our manner daring anyone to come between us. No one did. What a feeling! No one who hasn't been with a bunch of guys walking down the streets of their own turf can possibly understand the way I felt, and we all felt. Not once in our lives had any of us walked down a street and not felt burdened by the color of our skin and all that it represented. But the beauty of the feeling that I'm talking about is in the fact that we were black, and *powerful* to boot. Able as any white policeman to be supremely important, supremely unapproachable in the ghetto, to make folks cringe and get out of your way, to kill with a look, to know that though you are hated, you are feared even more.

We made a swaggering John Wayne entrance into the pool

hall, looked around the room, strolled over to the bar, then, with our backs to the bar, once again looked over the room like kings surveying their domain. And we didn't particularly like it when no one paid us any attention.

On the whole, it was a better than average pool-hall–bar, otherwise it wouldn't have had the girl there. She was playing an upright piano in a small alcove off to the left.

She was their attempt at class.

Without her, it was just a joint with five tables. But unlike the OK Pool Parlor the tables were good. Big money was bet here, and the only junkies who could get in were those who weren't known.

There was a high-stakes game in progress on one of the tables that riveted everyone's attention like a black Go-Go dancer in an all-white bar. The clicking of the balls as they struck each other and rebounded off the cushions framing the table was crisp, and even provided a certain pleasant accompaniment to the pretty voice of a pretty girl singing softly in the lounge area. Smoke drifted through the room along with the sweet smell of talcum powder, abetted by the perfume of the woman.

The two pool hustlers at the high-stakes table hoarsely called out bets, and circled in for shots. They played Chicago, a hard-slamming rotation game, which allowed the shooter virtually anything he could sink, so long as he hit his allotted ball first. The best strategy in Chicago was, therefore, to shoot with force and pick up extra balls on the hard-banking rebounds. The result was a roaring, crashing game. The room shook with the angry crack of ball on ball, the groans and shouts of the players, the tumultuous din of pitched battle.

Most eyes absorbed the action on the gambling table and reflected interest as the balls rolled, spun and slammed into the six pockets of the table. The eyes of the bettors pleaded as the mouths beneath them muttered cries of joy or raucous curses depending on whose balls sank or missed. The general atmosphere and the lights hanging brightly above the tables gave the impression of a boxing arena. All it lacked was the crunching cartilage and breaking jaws.

Vito Morese, a short, heavy-set, oily-haired hustler, sat on the edge of his seat with a thin Italian cigar held tightly between his lips. His breath could be heard issuing strongly through his hawklike nose as he watched his opponent preparing a shot. I saw that Vito was obviously winning and feeling good about it. He had a big meaty face with eyes that appeared mere slits cut into it. Smoke seemed to hang very heavy about him as his belly hung heavy upon him. He got up to sink the last ball into the side pocket and win the game.

Vito's opponent wanted to play another game. "Lemme get even. I lost twenty bucks."

"C'mon, Joey," Vito responded. "Ya got no more money. I know ya got no more. And if I win I'm gonna be awful mad at ya."

"I got money," Joey protested. "C'mon an play."

Vito pulled out about a hundred dollars. "Put up," he demanded.

"It's home. I'll pay ya when we finish playin."

Vito pocketed his money. "Naw."

"Ey, Vito. *C'maw!*"

"Ey, Joey. I said *naw!*" He look around the room, threw a kiss at the girl playing and singing, then shouted: "Anybody else feel lucky?"

It didn't occur to me to play him until no one else accepted his challenge. I'd seen him play before and believed that I had a better game than he. I turned to Mojo. "How much bread y'all got, man?" I asked.

Between us we had twenty-five dollars and some change. I called out to Vito, "Hey, man. I'll play you."

After looking me over he said, "Naw. I don't play wid you

guys. Most of youse was born in poolrooms." That got a few laughs and a few grumbles.

"Thought you said 'anybody,' man?" I shot back in the most contemptuous tone I could summon. "If you scared to play 'anybody,' don't challenge everybody; people might think you mean it."

That got a few approving murmurs and Vito's Italian complexion got nearly as dark as mine—which is saying a taste, if you know what I mean.

I turned to the girl. "Play a funeral march, baby. This cat's life on this table just came to an end." I threw her a kiss as I'd seen him do. "He died of fright," I added.

Vito exploded. "That's my girl you're talking to, fella. Don't t'row kisses at'er."

"Don't fool her into thinkin she's goin with a winner then," I taunted.

Vito stared at me. I could see his neck begin to bulge out over his collar and his lips got very wet. It was obvious that he found me even more odious than my blackness. His black, curly hair seemed to frizzle a bit and his hands tightened on the cue-stick they held. No one needed to ask what he wanted to do with it.

At last he said, "Whatcha wanna play for, *boy?*"

"Ten dollars a game, *Mister boy,*" I retorted.

"Rack em up then," he ordered the houseman. Then to me he said, "Put up in advance. We don't play on ass around here."

Pulling out ten dollars I said, "You ought to, there's more than enough of them here." We both gave our money to the houseman to hold and the game got under way.

When Vito broke the balls and ran only one of them, missing his second easy shot, my confidence soared. I ran off six of my balls before I missed. And I used the pool hustler's tactic of talking to one's opponent so as to irritate and distract him. Actually I didn't even need to talk to him because I knew he was out-classed even if he didn't.

Vito ran a couple of balls then missed again, leaving me an easy out. I knocked in the eight ball and won. My troops and a number of others who didn't care for Vito cheered. I think that by now everyone sensed that the game was for more than money.

The second game went much as the first had. Vito took a multitude of dumb shots and left himself no position when he did make one. When I wasn't shooting I was singing along with the girl, Sheila, and even walked over to the piano a few times to suggest a tune. She was affable but apprehensive. Entertaining the customers was her job, but Vito was her man, therefore, she was caught in the middle of a sticky situation.

Someone handed Vito a beer. His big hand almost hid it completely, and he nearly crushed it as he fumed over my attention to his girl. I was standing near her singing and watching him when, after taking a healthy swallow, he shouted:

"Whyn't you just play the game, fella, and stop talkin? You're gettin on my nerves wid all dat runnin off at the mouth."

I tried to make my smile innocent. "That's the way I play, man. I can't play no other way. Better you be nervous than me."

A voice called from the crowd: *"Let'em talk Vito. He ain't gonna win the money. Just let'em yak away."* It was a hopelessly hopeful voice.

I came over and sunk the twelve ball, then looked in the direction of the voice and gave a big grin. I only had one more ball to go, but I was so full of myself that I missed it. Even so, it was apparent that Vito couldn't win. He drained his beer and threw the empty can into the wastebasket.

105

My seeming nonchalance about the game and my interest in his girl were having their desired effect upon Vito. He couldn't keep his mind on the game nor his eyes from following me each time I missed and headed for Sheila and the piano. Vito made a few balls and his cheering section rode high on every push of the stick. I wasn't worried about him cheating because my troops kept a close watch on the table. I was oblivious to his menacing looks at me.

Once, when I saw him looking my way, I whispered to Sheila. The effect on Vito was marvelous. He missed his shot and cursed; then he banged his stick so hard against the table that it broke in half. I nearly doubled over with laughter. Then, walking to the table, I said:

"You shoot a pretty powerful stick, Vito baby. Too bad you don't do the same on *top* of the table." I shot and won the game. On the next rack I made the eight ball on the break, winning again. I taunted steadily:

"Houseman, houseman, rack'em fast,
I'm gon make this whuppin last!"

When this drew laughs I continued:

"Rack'em houseman, make it quick,
watch Vito break another stick!"

More laughs and even more anger from Vito.

While the balls were being racked up I moved off toward the piano again where Sheila was playing. "Hey, girl!" I called out. "Play that last number again. I'm gon sing it with you."

"*Hey!*" Vito shouted loud enough to drown out any sound in the place. His humiliation was more than he was going to take with sealed lips. He'd long ago lost his confidence and his backers could plainly see as much, and had ceased to bet on him. My troops were beaming and readily awaiting any action that might follow. "Somebody tell that nigger t'c'mon and play the game. I'm sick of him lollygaggin around!"

He spoke loud and no one had any trouble understanding what he had said. A hush fell over the place. I stopped in my tracks and slowly turned to face him. I guess my smile was frozen on my face because the muscles in my cheeks began to ache with a dry stiffness; I think the skin would have broken had I tried to change my expression. As I looked at Vito I don't believe he really knew what he had said, I mean, I could damn near forgive the guy because what he'd said seemed almost second nature to him. I even felt a tinge of remorse mixed with amusement at his helplessness.

Then he finally bent down to shoot again, satisfied that he had my attention if he couldn't have his victory. A funny feeling was slithering up from my groin, then reversed itself to creep down through my thighs and on down farther to the tips of my toes. It was a pins-and-needles kind of feeling that seemed to burst its way suddenly up into my brain. I walked back toward the table without feeling my feet touch the floor. It was like I was numb from the waist down. I stood over Vito as he prepared to shoot. He looked up at me.

Softly I heard my own voice as if from far back inside my head saying: "What'd you say, man?" It sounded tinny and unnatural like it wasn't me speaking at all.

He heard no warning in my voice, nor saw any threat in my close presence. Probably the farthest thing from his mind was that this black man would attempt to hurt him on his own turf. He stood up straight, looking down at me. I could smell, or thought I could smell, all of the Italian food he'd ever eaten oozing from the pores of his skin.

"I said c'mon and play the game. You heard me loud and clear."

I looked up at him. "What'd you call me, man?"

Vito looked puzzled. "What'd ya mean, 'what'd I call ya?' What're you talkin about?"

In evenly spaced tones I said, "Would you repeat exactly what you said?" I didn't take my eyes from his.

Still slightly perplexed Vito said, "Sure, I'll repeat it." He turned toward his cheering section and shouted: "Would somebody tell that nigger to c'mon and play the game. I'm sick of him lollygaggin around!" He turned to me. "And I am! So what's with you?"

"Nuthin, man," I said as casually as I could. "Ain't nuthin the matter with me." The feeling was again moving up through my torso; my neck felt gagged as the feeling bit its way through to my head. I turned and walked away and he bent to his shot.

I had no idea what I was going to do until I reached the spot where Vito's broken cue-stick lay. I stared at it a moment, then picked up the heavy part. The few who watched me pick it up said nothing, but most were intent on Vito's next shot. I took the few steps back to the table with an air of indifference—and, indeed, I felt no anger. But then, as I watched Vito shooting his shot, the prickly feeling exploded inside my head, and I brought the heavy end of the stick down across Vito's kidneys with a loud *thock!* that broke my calm.

He crashed to the floor as I whammed him twice more with the stick on his back and ribs that told all within earshot that something had to be broken—and it wasn't the stick. Vito curled up into a knot and moaned up at me from beneath the futile protection of his arms.

"Please, no more!" he begged. "Please, Shadow, *don't hit me again!*"

"Oh!" I said in mock surprise. "You *do* know my name, huh? I thought it was *boy*"— *Whack!* I hit him again. "I thought it was *nigger*"— *Slam!* I laid another blow across his outstretched arm so hard that he quickly shoved the arm between his legs. Tears were streaming from his red eyes as the full blast of all my hatred for him and whites and blacks both who had humiliated me in one way or another spun my senses so that I could hardly focus my eyes upon him. I could, however, clearly discern the blood that gushed forth from his mouth and nose, and a knot had jumped up on his head from a blow that I didn't remember giving him.

Ahmad and Mojo came over and pulled him out of my reach, and I seemed glued to the spot where my feet were planted, unable to follow and administer more punishment. Cootie, like a loyal follower, stood at my back. Even in my mental turmoil, though, I knew he was doing it in order to protect himself, for if anything happened to me his behind would also be in a sling.

My troops were by my side. We watched warily as Vito was helped to one of the benches alongside the room. He tried to clutch all the places on his body that hurt at once and failed miserably. His voice was fraught with pain as he asked: "What'sa matter with you? Why'd you hit me like that?" The cat was genuinely confused. I mean, he didn't seem to know what he had said. And immediately I was sorry for his stupidity—almost as much as I was aware of my own. In a flash I knew that this was what I had been secretly planning since we'd first entered the pool hall, or something similar to it. I looked at Vito and let my anger dissipate my momentary awareness.

"Listen, muthafucka," I said through clenched teeth. "I been a nigga baby, and I been a nigga boy, but I ain't gon be no nigga man for you or nobody else! You hear that, you fuckin punk?!"

Before he could answer we heard the wail of a siren off in

the distance. "That's the police," Mojo warned. "We better split."

"Yeah," Ahmad agreed. "And he prob'ly got a brother takin the call . . ."

Even as they led me out of the door I heard Vito's dazed voice saying: "What'sa matter with him? That nigger must be crazy! What'd he hit me for?"

Someone said: "You called him a nigger, Vito."

With sincere bemusement in his voice Vito said, "Well, what the hell is he? Ain't that what he is? If he ain't a nigger, what *is* he?"

I turned to look at him as he gestured to those listening to him: "I swear that nigger must be crazy! I didn do nothin t'im. You all saw it. I didn do nothin! That nigger is just crazy, that's what!"

My troops and I beat it around the corner before the patrol car pulled up. I felt it safer not to go home tonight.

11

I NEEDN'T have worried about the police because I saw one of the guys who'd been at the pool hall and he told me that Vito hadn't given my name to the police. I worried, however, that he would seek a personal vengeance. I mean, he was an Italian, and maybe he had Mafia connections. I had visions of myself stuffed in a barrel of lime in the Meadowland swamps, or floating stiff and bloated in the Passaic River—until it occurred to me that Vito was a five-and-dime Italian with about as much chance of getting Mafia help as me. He was nothing, and didn't have the price of a penny numbers hit, much less that of a hit-man.

In any event, I stayed inside all the next day. The following afternoon my troops came by to see if I was going with them to visit Sam in the hospital. I told them I had other plans.

"It's time we started thinkin about finances," I said. "I'm workin out a way to git some. How many guns y'all got?"

Mojo answered, "One. And we only got three bullets for it."

"What kind is it?" I asked.

"A .45," Cootie announced. "We shot at a coupla cops one night."

Ahmad corrected, "*I* shot at them. You was busy runnin."

"Well, shit," Cootie defended. "What the hell you expect? Them cats was hot on our case, man."

"Never mind all that," I interrupted. "Git a coupla more guns by tomorrow so that we'll all have one, cause tomorrow night we gon do some ridin. Is the car in shape?"

"It will be," Mojo assured me.

"Good. Have it ready."

"What we gon do?" Cootie wanted to know.

"I'll tell ya tomorrow before we do it."

After they left I turned on a soul-station and let disc-jockey bullshit engulf my brain. Then I thought about what I'd have us do tomorrow. It wasn't easy being a leader. That was becoming increasingly apparent. I got up, pulled off my pants and shirt and then lay back down.

The music, especially when the radio blasted out with James Brown screams, immediately brought back to me the times when Terri and I would lie here listening and dancing to the sounds. I didn't want to start thinking about her. I really didn't; and I tried my damnedest not to. But I was helpless in the matter. The more effort I put into not thinking the more strong the memories became; and impressions of her shook my consciousness. And worse, I began to feel sexually aroused. My johnson got as hard as a frozen peppermint stick.

I got up and poured myself a water tumbler full of wine, then returned to my bed. Man, I wanted some sex badly, and I wanted Terri especially. But I knew that I wasn't going to have her. I considered going out someplace and getting my needs satisfied by somebody's daughter, but seemed to lack the physical strength to make the effort. Forget sleep, though; there was no way the sandman, in my present state, could even dare approach me.

Now this may seem funny, but it's true nevertheless. I mean, dig. Before I knew it I was masturbating. I mean, one minute I was just lying there, resting my hands across my stomach, then my hand was innocently touching my johnson through the fabric of my shorts and the next thing I knew I was sitting up on the side of the bed sweating, eyes banged shut, while the image of Terri's pussy inundated every one of my senses. Like, I knew I was jerking-off, and I wanted to stop. I really did. But I couldn't bring myself to do so. I watched my johnson filling my hands as if they both belonged to someone else . . .

And those big, creamy thighs opened, and I saw through those fine, wispy hairs the white and the pink and the lush red that was Terri's cunt. Beautiful, beautiful. People have said that pussies are in fact ugly. Terri's wasn't ugly. I appreciated her pussy—no matter what else, I appreciated it. I mean, dig it: The sculpture of those two delicately molded mounds that framed the whole of her joy-box simply surrounded the essence of me. Like, I could see myself gently easing them apart and viewing—as if looking through the gates of heaven—how smoothly red and wet she was on the inside. . . . And is it so wrong to see myself that way? Watching my thumbs push upward and apart to allow her little pinkish clitoris to stick out its conical head and issue its taunting challenge; it was shiny and firm, and seemed even a bit coquettish.

Coming was anticlimactic, for the real beauty lay in the memory, the sensual pleasure of that memory, rather than in the act of coming itself. And even so, a huge and heavy sadness overcame me. I mourned the waste of solid and precious energy, which ought to have filled her being, as it plopped like a soggy dishrag onto my unscrubbed floor.

I fell back on the bed smelling the stink of my drying sweat and feeling very sorry for myself. There was only one consolation: now I could at least go to sleep and forget everything for a while.

The problem of what to do to create some action for my troops still faced me in the morning when I woke up. I was also supposed to go to work. I resolved that dilemma right away: I would quit my job. I just wasn't going to work anymore. My work from now on would be the revolution.

I got up, made some instant coffee, and tried to think of something for us to do. It would have to be dramatic, I knew. I discarded an attack on the police in favor of obtaining money. The latter would probably be more satisfactory to the others anyway; it was a more immediate and tangible enjoyment—and a lesser risk. There was a liquor store on Prince Street that would be ideal for a test and a nerve-builder for subsequent raids we would make on the capitalist coffers of the black community. The more I thought about it the better I liked the idea.

Now I'm not saying I had nerves of steel, and that robbery was easy. But any black man is capable of hard action when you get down to it. I'd known dozens of working stiffs who'd done the same, straight dudes who one day packed it in and picked up the gun. Dig, more than any other people we live out our fantasies, especially the violent ones—murder, robbery, rape, the stark reality we live with.

So maybe nerves of steel weren't required after all. Maybe my life had been programed to deal with it in advance. One day I was a straight cat, waiting for old age and social security, the next day I was picking up the gun. It was all the same, all part of the same crumby package—not exactly easy, but I could live, even die, with it.

And why not? maybe I figured. We kick our woman's ass when we're bugged at the job. We destroy our children's lives. We stab, cut and shoot each other in our fury, and then apologize to the white cop who arrests us, all the time revealing how shallow and empty our anger is. Why shouldn't we re-route the rage?

After their daily visit to Sam at the hospital my troops came to my pad. "We could only git one gun besides the one we already got," Mojo regretted.

By way of explanation Ahmad added: "Sam's mother's boyfriend got the other one we was gon git, but we didn't have no way of gittin it cause Sam ain't home."

"Yeah," Cootie continued. "He got a bitchy mutha, who don't trust nobody—specially us. She reactionary."

"What about yo momma?" Ahmad teased. "She just as bad."

Cootie became angry. "Don't talk about my mutha, man. I don't play the dozens."

"That's enough," I ordered. "At least we got two pieces. That oughta be cool for what we gotta do."

In unison they asked, "What is it?"

"The Prince Liquor Store."

"When we gon do it?" Ahmad wanted to know.

"Tonight."

Mojo was apprehensive. "Ain't that a black liquor store?"

"What you mean 'black'?" I stared back at him.

"Black dude owns it, don't he?"

I gave him a long, searching look. "You the one who spozed to be the hippest on revolutionary tactics and rhetoric, man. You the one who claim that the only thing a poor man can lose is his life, cause he ain't got nuthin else . . ."

"Yeahm, but—"

"But my butt!" I cut in. "The dude don't own *nuthin,* so we ain't robbin him."

Cootie caught Mojo's feeling. "Man, we oughta take off some white dudes first. They the biggest capitalists."

I was becoming fast frustrated with these cats. "Listen, sucka," I addressed myself to all of them. "Y'all's the same muthafuckas who was spoutin all that shit about black people not ownin a fuckin thing in this country. Blacks don't mint no money; they don't own no land or anything that comes out of it. Y'all agree that the goddamn cracker can rip it off anytime—like they did the Japs. So niggas only rent the land. Niggas drink as much liquor as anybody, but they ain't got one fuckin distillery—not to mention a distributorship. So what the hell y'all mean by sayin it's a black store? Is y'all outa yo dialectical minds? It's a capitalist establishment killin off the people with rotgut!"

They all looked at me in mild shock, and I wondered if, in the weeks that we'd been together, I had changed that much. I mean, I had secretly felt myself outgrowing them, but I didn't know that it showed. And, after all, it was their logic I was using. I drove on.

"Who's the enemy of the people?" I asked.

"The capitalist Establishment and their running-dog lackeys!" Mojo answered.

"What color is the enemy?"

"The enemy comes in all colors!"

"So," I continued. "Is that so-called black store owned by the people or an enemy of the people?"

"It's owned by an enemy of the people!"

I allowed myself a smile of triumph. "Nuff said then."

We waited until near closing time. There weren't many people on Prince Street, but there were enough so that it wasn't deserted. I thought that was good since if the cops happened upon us they might be a little less inclined to start shooting. We drove past the store a couple of times, checking things over and gulping down the Seagrams we had brought along with us. I don't mind admitting that I needed the extra nerve it seemed to give to me. I had no doubt that the others needed it, also.

Ahmad was driving. I rode shotgun while Mojo and Cootie sat in back.

"Any more of the whiskey left?" Mojo wanted to know as we pulled to the curb half a block away from the store.

"No," I said. "Why?"

"I could stand another taste, too," Cootie put in.

Ahmad grunted his agreement. I said nothing for a moment then, in a cutting, contemptuous tone, designed to hide my own fear, I said, "What's the matter? Y'all got the jitters or somethin?" Before anyone could respond I was getting out of the car.

"I'll walk down there and git a bottle. Give me a chance to look the place over better."

I walked away from them as casually as I could. I knew they were watching me closely and I hoped my cool wouldn't be betrayed by the slight but uncontrollable trembling in my knee-joints.

Three customers were inside the place. That made five people to handle, with the owner and his clerk. I bought our jug with an air of nonchalance, carefully trying to see if anyone else was in the back room. I saw no one. Back outside I breathed deeply of the night air; it filled my lungs and kind of eased the oppressive feeling that seemed to want to crush me. I mean, I was feeling as though every window in that block had someone looking out at me just waiting to be called as a witness to what we were about to do. Man! Even as I'd bought the whiskey I found that I couldn't look the man in the eye for fear that he'd see "stick-up man" written all over my face. It was strange that, as much as I'd drunk, I wasn't the least bit high. I mean, it seemed that the more I drank the more sober I became. I couldn't loosen the tightness that gripped my chest, or stem the thumping of my heart.

To reach the car again finally was as satisfying as climbing into my warm bed after a particularly tiring day at the factory. Hell, I think it even felt better.

After opening the bottle and taking a healthy swig, I said, "Ain't but three customers and two workers in the place. Drink up fast and let's move."

All of us got out except Cootie. He jumped behind the wheel.

"Whatchoo spozed t'be doin, man?" I asked.

"Somebody gotta drive and play chickee, don't they?"

I opened his door. "You git the fuck outa there and come with us! Everybody's goin in. Just leave the motor runnin. When we git in you hit the cash register; the rest of us'll hold the people."

We reached the door just as one of the customers was leaving. It was too late to allow him to go. Shoving him back inside Mojo announced:

"Okay, everybody, this is it. Stick'em up!"

We moved in waving our guns and herding the people against the counter. Cootie surprised me by his speed in getting to the register. He had it open and was stuffing his pockets when a woman came from somewhere in the back. When she realized what was happening she let out the loudest scream I'd ever heard.

"Eeeeeee!" she shrieked. *"Help! Police! Police! We's bein robbed agin!"* She took off back to where she'd been, screaming like all the devils in hell were after her.

We, of course, were startled near witless. And in our confusion must have taken our eyes off our victims because the next thing I knew I was grabbed from behind and flung to the floor. Then I heard shots being fired. I struggled against the man who had grabbed me as he held on for dear life. Even though I banged him over the head with my pistol he wouldn't let go of me. We rolled over the floor amid shots and screams.

"Let's git the hell outa here!" somebody shouted.

I heard footsteps pounding toward the door. Panic must have given me strength because I threw the man off me. My senses were reeling with excitement; anxiety flooded my whole body so that even when I regained my footing I had no sense of direction. I found myself running toward the counter instead of the door. The owner had gotten hold of a gun and was kneeling down behind the counter firing wildly up at the ceiling. All I could see was his hand holding the gun as he sent shot after shot into the plaster overhead. I fired at the bottle behind him. I could not have hit him if I wanted to because I couldn't see him. He must have been as afraid as I was. I wanted him to stay that way, at least until I could get out of there.

Wheeling about, I headed for the door. I saw the man who had grabbed me and my fear vanished for a fraction of a second to be replaced by anger. I don't recall that I stopped running, but I remember the utter shock on his face as I pointed the gun directly at him. His hands went up as if to ward off the bullet and his mouth opened without emitting any sound. My head was so full of so many indistinguishable sounds, as if I were carrying around a thousand echo chambers within me, that I couldn't have heard him anyway.

I pulled the trigger but the gun was empty, empty as my momentary anger. Then fear and the craving to escape returned to me with all its passion. My troops were long gone and the bastards had closed the door behind them. As I started for it, I glanced back to see the owner climbing over his counter, the .45 in his hand. It went off and a fifth of Old Grand-Dad exploded just above my head, the wet, sweetish bourbon soaking my neck, broken glass falling on my shoulders and face.

There was no time to open the door now. I closed my eyes and went right over the window display, through shelves of liquors and wines and then through the store's front windowpane. I landed outside amid a shower of broken bottle shards and shattered glass. I slipped once, but was on my feet and running for all I was worth toward the car. My shoulder felt like someone had hit it with a 60-ounce Louisville Slugger and and my face seemed to be bitten by a hundred stinging mosquitoes.

As I climbed into the car Ahmad screeched away from the curb burning rubber, squalling and swerving wildly to avoid hitting a drunk who picked that moment to cross the street in front of us. I had just made it inside the car. Now I looked back to see if the drunk was attempting to get our license-plate number. To my relief he was looking in the opposite direction, shaking his fist at what he must have thought was us.

"Head for my place," I told Ahmad.

"You alright?" Mojo looked me over with a frown.

"Shoulder hurts from hitting that goddamn hard glass," I said.

Cootie was looking at me wide-eyed. "Man, you cut up!"

"Well then, git me the fuck home so I can see how bad!" I shouted.

120

When we got to my house, being careful not to be seen, I immediately removed all my clothes in order to check the damage I had done to myself. With the exception of a deep gash on my left leg, right arm, and the hellish pain in my shoulder, I was okay. There were small cuts on my face, but they were the least of my worries.

We tended my wounds as best we could: washing and dabbing with alcohol and iodine until the stinging had my eyes filled with tears. It took a long time to stem the flow of blood from my leg but it, too, finally ceased. I was nauseous, dizzy and weak—but not insensible enough to forget about the money, especially since Cootie was holding it.

"Three hundred and eighty-seven dollars," he proudly responded to my query. "And I got us a quart of Jack Daniel whiskey, too." He opened it, took a long drink and damn near choked himself into a faint. I felt as good about that as I had about getting away from the liquor store.

I think we were all a little angry at him for the same reason: had he been alert instead of just looting, perhaps that woman wouldn't have surprised us. No one, however, voiced the thought and I was feeling too weak and relieved to care. We had, after all, made it.

Softly, as if through a dense mesh of fog, I heard Mojo asking for a drink of the Jack Daniels. Their voices came and went as I drifted into unconsciousness:

Ahmad: "Man, did y'all see the way brutha Shadow come through that glass window . . ."

Cootie: "Wowie! That nigga outdid a *Shaft* movie. Why I betcha he . . ."

I was gone.

12

STAYING IN the house only made me want Terri all the more. I couldn't rid myself of even the smallest memory of her. I felt that there had to be some way out of my turmoil, but every exit seemed inexorably closed to me.

In a few days the little scars on my face were well healed; though my left leg and arm still pained the hell out of me I was able to limp around. During my convalescence my troops were as faithful to me as they were to Sam. They came to my pad every day with a gallon jug and a quart of Seagrams (our intake had increased with our prosperity) and we'd make plans about our next revolutionary moves. It was only after some wine mellowed within me that I began drifting in my head away from tactics to Terri.

It was on Saturday afternoon that I decided to call her. I

hobbled down to the corner confectionery store and, with trembling fingers, dialed her number.

"Hello?" It was her voice, softer and sweeter than I recalled.

An almost unmanageable fear gripped me and I nearly hung the receiver back in its cradle. What, after all, was I going to say to her? I mean, after the way I had treated her the last time we were together, what could she want to say to me except "later, chump"?

"Hello . . . ?" she repeated.

I disguised my voice, making it much deeper than it normally is. "Is this Terri?" I asked.

"Yes . . ."

"I'm a friend of Shadow's," I hurried on. "He been hurt pretty bad and been askin for you."

Her voice went brick hard. "What does he want?"

I was disappointed that she didn't ask how bad I was hurt or anything. But I was also glad because I couldn't have answered and might have stumbled into blowing my cover.

"I don't know what he want," I said. "But I think you oughta go see'im. He in rough shape, from what I hear."

"Well, that's too bad. I'm sorry, but I won't be able to see him. Is he in the hospital?"

My heart sank. Man, if a cat can't play on a woman's sympathy he's really in trouble.

"That's just it," I improvised. "He should be in the hospital, but he won't go. He won't say nuthin except that he needs to die for the way he treated you."

"That's right," she retorted hoarsely.

Now that response really destroyed my hopes. What can you say to a bitch who says something like that about you—and behind your back, too?

"What's wrong with him?" she asked at length. I was sure

that I'd heard a slight softening of her tones. It wasn't a decibel less determined, just softer. Inquisitive, if you will. My hopes underwent a revival.

"He fell through a glass window and got cut up," I said.

"Did he say why he wanted to see me?"

"No, he didn't. He don't even know I'm callin you."

Her questions were making me see double. I could have screamed at her to say something positive, one way or the other. Finally—and her voice was softer still, I knew it beyond a doubt—she asked:

"Is he at home?"

"Yeah," I said. "But don't tell him I called you, hear?"

Her voice was hard again. "I don't even know who you are. And I didn't say I was going to see him!"

"Well, from the way he talked about you I guess I just assumed you would. I mean, I don't know what happened between y'all, but—"

"All right," she cut in. "Never mind the soft soap. I'll come by his place later on tonight—just to see how he is."

I couldn't possibly describe my joy as I hung the phone up. I know I had a silly battered smile on my face. There were some kids in the store, hanging around the candy counter. I took out a dollar bill, gave it to the man who ran the store, and told him to give them what they wanted. Then I left the store whistling a joyful snatch of music.

The street seemed particularly bright and cheery as I made my way back home. Sure, it was the same old street on which I'd grown up. The filthy tenements, the urinous stoops, the empty, littered lots, the rotting projects—it was all the same. Strung-out junkies, slobbering drunks, shrieking kids, and broken-down adults, but somehow in my temporary insanity I saw them all differently. Don't get me wrong, it wasn't all due to Terri. I mean, of course she had something to do with it. But the feelings I had went beyond her. Like, there was something in the way certain people I passed greeted me. Hip folks who used to give me a wide berth were digging me, as well as the usual working stiffs.

I came to Mrs. Gladys Johnson's house, which was a few buildings from where I lived. Hers was a first-floor walk-through and she seemed to have nothing to do except to sit and look out of her window, day and night. In the summer she'd lean out so far that you could touch her as you passed. She was huge, man, with circus-tent dresses, breasts like beach-balls, and fat-rippling arms that she braced herself with on her window ledge.

And in the winter hers was the cleanest window on the block. She rubbed it day and night keeping it clear of mist so that she could peer out. I don't remember ever having passed without seeing her. She also had an ugly daughter with whom she was forever trying to involve me, along with any other young man she deemed worthy, which meant he had a job and didn't give her any sass when she was being nosy.

I saw her as I passed by. "Hellow, Miz Johnson!" I called.

She gave me a look worthy of Medusa. She then turned her face away as if she hadn't heard me (as if she missed anything that was said on that block, and indeed, in most of the neighborhood).

Determined to get a reply, I stopped. "Hi, Miz Johnson. How you do?"

She leveled the evil eye. "Yew jes get from the fronta me, boy. I heard about'choo. Yew done turned inta a no-count nigga lak da ress'a'm!" She banged her window shut.

But if some of the squares ducked me, the hip folk drew close. My notoriety enhanced their stature. My troops had spread the word of our exploits, and lots of the neighborhood gang had heard. For instance, Johnny Frank, that same cat who'd disapproved of Terri and told me that his commitment to the black race came through the head of his dick, came up to me and offered me some of his wine.

"Hey, my main man, Shadow!" he roared. "What's happnin, baby? Ain't seen you for a good taste." He shoved his bottle into my hand. And others, whom I'd only known on sight, called to me as if we'd been the most bosom of buddies.

"Hey, man you a livin legend!"

"Yeah, baby! We been hearin boutcha."

"Dig it, Shadow! How's it shakin?"

It was fame and I accepted it. "Y'all ain't heard nuthin yet," I'd reply evenly.

I was cool, distant. They caught my chill and more important sensed that I didn't want them to speak on what they'd heard. I moved away.

"Don't spread no rumors, man. That's how people come to jails and graves."

I had better things on my mind and I hurried along as best I could. The first thing I did upon reaching my pad was to tidy the joint up a bit. There wasn't much that could be done with it, but I did what I could. Then I wrapped more gauze around my arm and leg. I needed the sympathy thing going for me. Then I finally settled down to wait for Terri, although my state of mind could hardly be called settled.

I turned on the radio—no James Brown this time but slow easy soul—and lay down as the last light of day stretched itself away over the roofs of the projects, tenements and the old Krueger Brewery. I guess I meditated on my cracked ceiling and my crimson bulb, but I don't recall my thoughts, except those of Terri. I wondered what I would say. I even rehearsed some things that I'd gotten from the movies. Nothing stayed with me because, though my expectations of her visit ran from Newark to the tip of the Himalayas, I wasn't sure that she'd show up.

Her knock, when it came, was soft, but it flailed my ears like a thunderclap. I hurriedly climbed beneath the covers.

"Come in," I whimpered, trying to sound ill but not succeeding too well. I was about to repeat it when she entered wearing a yellow, ruffled blouse with a white pleated skirt, which with all that white skin made her look like a saffron princess floating out of the pages of a fairy tale. I tried to concentrate on her face, to read it if I could, but the totality of the vision overwhelmed me. It was as though I felt her essence, plumbed the bottom of her soul. With all the breath in my lungs I wanted to shout that I loved her—would forever love her, no matter what. I wanted her to know and feel the depths to which I felt those words. She would know me then. She would know my need. She would know my dreams. And she would know what to do.

I said nothing. I let her speak first. Her voice wasn't hard; it had no anger in it. "Someone called me today. He said you asked for me."

"I didn't know," I whispered back. "I didn't tell anybody to call . . . I didn't think you'd come anyway . . ."

Like undisputed royalty she perched on my ragged armchair. And I was sure she knew the caller had been me. If she hadn't known before, she did know now. We looked at each other, half-smiling, embarrassed, guilty, in the way that only two formally involved people can manage.

"How are you feeling now?" she asked.

"Fine," I replied.

"That's good. What happened to you?"

"Accident. I fell through a plate-glass window. I was stoned —I been stoned a lot since you left."

"I didn't leave. I was thrown out—remember?"

Her sarcasm wasn't lost on me. I felt it to the core. "I'm sorry for that," I said. "I been sorry for a lotta things since then."

She smiled. "Well, let's not deal with that. I only wanted to see how you were. The man on the phone made it seem like you were practically dead." She allowed herself an even broader smile.

I relaxed some. "You glad or sad?" I asked.

"Oh, now really. Why would I want you dead?"

I was only half-teasing when I said, "Would you want me —period?"

"What do you mean?"

I didn't feel up to playing this what-do-you-mean game. I knew that she was well aware of what I meant, but, typically, she needed the words. I guess none of us value feelings without words to accompany them. Yet I began, in the following moments, as we searched each other's faces, to sense something else going on between us. I mean, like, what about her need for me? After all the shit I'd put down on her, she was here with me. She certainly had power over me. But didn't her being here say something about the power I also had over her?

I said, "I ain't so dumb, Terri."

"I never said you were."

"Then why you wanna make me play dumb games?"

She opened her mouth as if to protest, but I silenced her with a raised hand. "Listen," I went on. "You know damn well what I mean."

The innocent look spreading over her features only increased the calm rage that simmered within me.

She said: "If you mean do I want you for you—as I wanted you before—the answer is no. I only came here for one reason: the concern of one human being for another . . ."

"You lyin!" My voice was strained rather than loud, and my throat was tightened by an unimaginable pressure. "You *know* you lyin!"

"What!"

"Shut up!" I hissed at her. "Don't you gimme non'a that white patronizin bullshit. Save it for them fuckin junkies . . ."

For a long time afterward we looked at each other. I had no way to gauge what she was thinking. I don't even remember what I thought. I only recall how drastically inadequate she made me feel. Why, I asked myself, was I like this with her. I mean, what was there about this woman that twisted my mind and stomach into one huge, bloating knot?

I broke the silence. "C'mere," I said.

"No."

I got up. She didn't move. "Come here," I repeated.

Her expression didn't change. "What for?"

"Because I said so."

She looked boldly at me. "That's no reason."

"Because I'm gon fuck you. Cause you mine."

She smiled. "That's a joke. No."

"Well, I ain't Bob Hope, goddammit!" I pulled her to her feet.

She began to struggle against me. "No! This isn't why I came here. Don't—"

"Woman, I'm gon fuck you!"

"No you're not! Now stop it and leave me alone!" She pulled away and headed for the door.

I grabbed her and flung her back toward the bed. "You ain't goin nowhere!"

As she fell back on the bed anger flashed and died in her eyes and a stoiclike calm spread over the rest of her features. "Are you going to rape me? Is that what you intend?"

"If that's what it takes. You mine."

"If I was yours you wouldn't have to take it."

"You gon give it to me then?"

"No," she said.

"Then I'm takin it—git undressed!"

She displayed curiosity—and a hint of disgust—in the cool manner with which she disrobed. And when she was before me in all her naked loveliness I couldn't miss the air of asexuality that draped her like a shroud. "Rape was our beginning, wasn't it?" she said.

I looked at her in silence. She stared right through me. "You won't enjoy this," she warned. "But then you didn't even enjoy it as a gift, did you? I won't help you this time. I won't even try."

I pushed her down on the bed. Watching her lie there emotionless as I removed my shorts gave me a strange sensation. I felt as though I didn't want her at all, and I began to sweat with the effort to concentrate on taking her anyway. Past memories of my futile attempts with her conflicted in my head with the tangible need I had for her, and I was lost amid the savage battle of desire and the lack of will. Her face was blank, but I know I felt her smirking at me.

I reached out to touch her. She pushed my hand away. I was attacked by a thumping in my chest. I reached out again and laid my hand on her heaving breasts. Again she pushed my hand away, much harder this time.

The thumping and the heat inside me grew. I felt something creeping down my leg. I thought it was a roach, but when I brushed at it I felt wetness. My leg had begun to bleed and I watched as the blood from my wound coursed down toward my ankle. I don't know why it bled. I hadn't hit it—at least I didn't remember doing so.

"Why don't you let me go?" Terri said. "You know it's no good. *I don't want you!*"

Suddenly the thumping stopped; my mind became a temporary void, but the heat within me burned higher and higher

130

until I found myself lying on top of her fighting to keep her from pushing me off. My determination increased with her struggling. It didn't occur to me to hit her. This was a battle of wills rather than blows.

"You don't want me, huh?" My breathing was a loud ocean in my ears. I heard my voice as if from a great distance repeating, *"You don't want me, huh?"*

Using more force than was actually necessary, I pinned her beneath me, pressing the full weight of my body down and forcing open her thighs. Even at that moment I thrilled at the soft malleableness of her thighs. Her muscles were taut under the soft meat as she tried to keep her legs together.

She had tightened up inside. Only the ramrod stiffness of my johnson enabled me to enter her. But even so, it only went in past the head. I began to move slowly, carefully, for fear that she would force me out. I pushed against her tightened walls until our struggle became a matter of whose muscles would relax first.

She relaxed first and I shoved inside causing her shallow breath to catch. She quickly renewed her efforts but it was too late. I was in to stay.

"Get off of me!" she hissed.

I concentrated all my energies on my task.

"You're no good!" she taunted. "You can't make it, you black bastard! I'll laugh at you when your prick falls—and it will! You know it will. You can't make it and I don't want you!"

But something was building inside me—and I knew the feeling. I knew that if my concentration held I would be justly rewarded. I threw everything out of my mind except the growing feeling. Still, the negative things she'd said to me crept in, but, strangely enough, they only served to stimulate me. It was a weird sensation. I mean, when she'd tried to please me I couldn't make it, but now that she was trying to discourage me I felt a surge of power equal to anything I'd ever felt before. Even though my concentration almost broke at the thought that I was some kind of freak, I held fast.

Abruptly the feeling enlarged itself until that moment arrived when a man knows he's going to come and nothing on earth can stop him. It was the moment when, almost imperceptibly, the meter changes and woman catches on to the beat that makes the act the universal phenomenon that it is. Terri's breath caught again, but this time it was with the thrill of grabbing a star.

The difference was there. I felt her moisture grow around me and her body grow wider in receptivity. Her satisfaction, however, was a distant thought in my head. It became more compelling, and the whooshing of hot-ice pinpointed every sensate area of my body. It was painful ecstasy to which I abandoned myself.

I throbbed inside and she too built toward climax. Now she was pleading with me to hold on until it arrived. A perverse thought seized me for a moment: I had the notion to jerk out of her and watch her squirm. I didn't do it.

"Please," she whispered, "oh, please don't stop. Let me . . . *Wait!* Let me . . ."

I lay on her, exhausted but proud, as she ground her body to mine. I wasn't concerned or fully aware of her. *I had done it!* I had come in her at last and the fascination with the fact enthralled me.

She finally did come, but it meant next to nothing to me. I rolled off and allowed the hot needles of my drying sweat to play out the end of my passion.

Neither of us said anything for a long time afterward. I had no urge to talk anyway. She lighted cigarettes and I couldn't help but notice the complete change in her attitude.

132

Again she was the Terri I'd first known. She cuddled close with her head on my shoulder while her free hand roamed my body. Every few minutes she would gently fondle my private parts with a sigh.

After a while I sat up in bed. "Is you mine now?" I asked.

"Oh, yes," she replied sweetly.

Someone knocked at my door. Terri grabbed my hand. "Don't answer it. Let's be alone."

I shook my head. "Who is it?" I called, knowing full well who it was.

A muffled voice came back. *"It's me—*Mojo!"

"Come back in bout an hour, man!"

"Okay, brutha." We listened to muffled footsteps going away.

There was mixed fear and perplexity assembling Terri's expression. "What's he want with you?" She asked.

"We doin some bizness together," I said. "You better git dressed."

She gave me a searching look before she rose to dress. I watched her with pleasure and satisfaction bubbling all through my body. She was putting her shoes on when I asked, "You wanna see me again?"

Standing, she said, "You know I do."

"Then I'll call you tomorrow."

"All right."

Still nude myself, I walked her to the door where we kissed.

"I want to touch it again," she said, taking my johnson into her hand. "It's finally become something real to me."

I laughed. "The answer to your dreams, huh?"

"No," she said. "My prayers."

13

"BRUTHA," MOJO smiled knowingly as he and Ahmad walked into my pad. "You was settin a helluva fire under whoever was in here with you. We couldn't help but hear what was goin down."

"Yeah, man," Ahmad added. "Who was it? She gon contribute to the revolution?" They both laughed.

"Never mind all that," I said. "What y'all want, and where's Cootie?"

"You got him stimulated and he went to his woman's house," Ahmad said. "I felt like gittin my own nuts outa the sand, too."

Mojo said—and he spoke slowly as though he'd been smoking pot—"We just came by t'see if you done planned our next move. Thought we'd check you out."

"I been thinkin on it," I said. "I ain't quite got it together yet, but it's comin sometime next week."

"Hey, by the way," Ahmad said. "Sam said t'tell you hello, and that he ain't mad at you no more. He may even be outa the hospital in time to git down with yo plans next week."

"That's cool with me. I ain't mad at him, either."

Mojo, taking a swig of leftover Grand-Dad, said, "Looka here, man. I mean, like, really—who was the babe you had here when we came back before?" Both of them were grinning at me in that snickering manner men reserve for sex-related ideas.

I didn't know if I wanted to tell them or not. I was caught between the desire to brag, to let them know that I had "gotten over," and the deep sacredness that seemed so much a part of my relationship to Terri. What to tell them, I suppose, was less important than how to tell them. There was a superfine line straight down the middle of my feelings for Terri, and I was none too sure how these guys would affect it because of my inability to properly relate it to them. I knew one thing though: it was important for them to understand that she was not just another woman, but it was equally as important for them to realize that that's all she was.

Ahmad, I guess because he was an ex-Black Muslim, would only accept her in theory, but his distrust and dislike of all white people stood between our understanding like the Great Wall of China. His Muslim background had provided him with a set of moral and historic examples, both real and imagined, that the rest of us lacked. And in talking with him about race a person found himself overwhelmed by the sheer weight of his "facts" about the "so-called white man." He was much better-read and better self-disciplined than any of us.

So I debated with myself a while before telling them about Terri, not because I couldn't have gotten them to accept the fact of my affiliation—and act accordingly—but because they wouldn't accept the idea of it; and the trust built between them and me couldn't have withstood the force of a spitball, given the right set of circumstances and the wrong point of view.

I finally decided to plunge right ahead and tell them, like it or not. I mean, after all, she was my woman. I wasn't going to have anybody telling me when, how or whom I should love. It was my own affair; I couldn't help it if others chose to make it theirs. No black woman had come close to fulfilling me as had Terri, and life was much too short to go around in the ghetto, like the Prince in Cinderella, looking for a black foot on which to place the slipper of my life. I was resolved to place it where it comfortably fitted—and fuck you, world.

"Before I tell you who it was," I said at last. "I want you cats to stop all the braggin in the neighborhood about what we done—especially when it involves robbery. I ain't ready t'go to jail. And make sure y'all tell Cootie the same thing, cause he prob'ly the one doin it to make hisself look big."

"I ain't told nobody," they each said.

"I ain't accusin nobody directly." I looked at both of them. "Just make sure it don't happen no more. Everybody'll know us when the time's right."

They nodded agreement as I rose to get us more Grand-Dad. Taking the first swig, I handed the bottle to Mojo.

"It was Terri," I hit them with it abruptly, careful to watch their reaction. "We done got back together, and I'ma try t'see it stays that way."

The only visible flinch came, as I knew it would, from Ahmad. His manner was outwardly calm and his voice held no tangible animosity as he said, "Can't find what you lookin for in a black woman, huh?" It wasn't a question, it was a challenge.

I remained as cool as he. "I ain't lookin no more. Why should I when I got what I need in this one—that make sense?"

"Does to me," Mojo said. Ahmad said nothing.

"Make sense to you, Ahmad?" I insisted.

136

He took a deep breath. "That depends on if you usin common sense or nigga sense—and I hope you don't take that the wrong way. I ain't tryin to insult you."

"What you tryin t'do then?" I asked, feeling quite insulted.

"I'm tryin t'wake up you and every other black man who lusts after dead white flesh and dead white values," he shot back. "Ain't nothin good in a white woman that a black woman ain't got more of."

Mojo jumped in: "Here we go again. Brutha, don't start that cat talkin bout white folks, he don't know when to quit."

I lit a cigarette. "Well, I think it's somethin that needs t'be brought out, if we gon have unity in our group."

"Well," Mojo replied. "I done heard it a million times, and he might be one hundred percent right about the white man, but can't him or nobody else tell me there's a difference between black and white pussy. I done had a lot of both, and if a bitch can fuck, she can fuck—and you better believe it, man."

Ahmad was momentarily peeved at Mojo. It was obvious that they'd had this confrontation before. "What I'm talkin about ain't got nuthin t'do with fuckin," he said.

"Same here," I agreed.

"Good!" he went on. "Because I'm talkin about the total idea of blacks and whites in this country and in most, if not all, of the Western world."

Again Mojo interrupted. "What's all them folks got to do with Shadow and his stuff?"

Ahmad looked as though he were a patient parent explaining a simple problem of logic to a child. "It's got nothing to do with him if not everything," he stated.

"That sounds heavy," I challenged. "But what do it mean?"

Ahmad turned toward me, reaching his hand out for the Grand-Dad. I gave it to him. "It means," he said, "that the *idea* of fallin in love with a white woman—given the world we live in—is wrong; and the *act* of fallin in love with one is a disaster—especially for somebody that the people look up to. Man, we traveled nowhere with them in peace since our two races first met and recognized a difference in our looks, and the distance from yesterday to tomorrow is so long that nobody will ever git from one point to the other. Nobody ever has. We all die before we can complete the journey. We oughta take that journey with our own kind. It's the only chance we got."

"Brutha Ahmad," Mojo said. "For the sake of argument, couldn't we bridge that gap?"

"No way. Nothing's strong enough. No chain's long enough. It'd take those already dead to form it, and that's impossible."

It was my turn to take the bourbon. "Man, then what's the point of us bein together? I mean, ain't we tryin to change things? Seems to me we oughta start with ourselves." I thought I had him with that.

Ahmad sneered wolfishly. "Yes, with our*selves!* But not with our open enemies. I got no objection to dealin with whites, after we've done the job of dealin with ourselves *first*. How we gon git together with people who don't like us because of our skin color, when we can't even git together with ourselves? Don't y'all see?"

Mojo and I looked at him for a long while without saying anything. My brain was so full of the need to reject what it had heard that it went blank and left me staring like an idiot.

"Looka here," Mojo said, "people is people."

Ahmad smiled again, the upper lip up. "All cats is cats, too, but you don't see no lions hangin out with panthers, do you?"

"People got brains," I said, "they can love. What about love?"

"What about it?" he asked.

138

"I love Terri. Is that wrong?"

"Love ain't never wrong, brutha."

"Then what—"

"But *who* you love can be wrong. And, really, we only love for selfish reasons anyway."

"What the hell you talkin about, man? Selfish! You gon keep on talkin till you hang yoself."

Ahmad stared balefully at me. "That's *yo* judgment, brutha-man. Love ain't nuthin. It simply is. It exists without explanation, like every other phenomenon of Nature, and it only survives through natural selection, the Law of self-preservation—it's selfish. Now don't let that word throw you, the selfish I'm talkin about ain't got nuthin t'do with the negative way we use the word. It don't mean a cat don't care about nuthin but hisself. That's too simple to even begin to explain what I mean. We love somebody, not because they deserve it so much, but because—and dig this—there's somethin about that person that makes us want to be loved by them. So, y'see, we love selfishly, because we feel *we* is deservin of love ourselves. It ain't good or bad until *we* say so; it ain't given or receivin until *we* determine it is. You can make all the judgments you want about it, man, but that don't mean you right."

Mojo must have seen my anger rising. "I told you not t'git him started," he cautioned. He then lit up a reefer, took in a lungful of smoke, held it and blew it out, groaning.

Ahmad seemed actually bored with us, and his attitude of benign superiority was a growing ball in my stomach.

"Man," I said at length. "What you sayin destroys the very foundations of love among individuals as well as among peoples."

"Is that so bad? Is those foundations so strong now? Maybe they oughta be destroyed so we can build better ones. I mean, shit, man, *you* the one with the problem of facin the fuckin world with yo love, not me. And it's the same world that gave you all that nonsense about love conquerin all obstacles. All that shit about truth and fidelity is the hypocrite, not me."

He seemed to become angry himself as he talked, and his anger didn't focus on myself or Mojo. He looked beyond us, perhaps to the trash-heap upon which lay his own idealism. In a flash I saw that his cynicism was really due to his disappointment with the world that had made him what he had become. He could never accept blame, because the world that made him was the same world that had condemned him. I seemed to see a cop-out in his attitude.

He took a small sip of the bourbon and continued. "Listen, we both know where we stand in relation to the world and the shit that's goin down around us everyday, but the difference between us is that I ain't gon apologize to the world for nuthin—and I certainly ain't gon apologize *for* it. I ain't got no time for white people because the needs of black people is too great."

"Anybody wanna smoke some'a this joint with me?" Mojo asked, oblivious to Ahmad's speech. "It's dynamite, baby."

I reached for it and pulled the smoke deep into my lungs, holding it there until my lungs were near collapse. Then I passed it to Ahmad, who refused it while pouring himself another drink.

"Dig, Ahmad," I said. "A while ago you said we all die before we can complete the journey—the distance from yesterday, as you called it. Well, if that's true, what's the use of anything? Why you so hot to change things? What's revolution?"

"Frankly, brutha, I don't know that it is true. I'm only diggin it from a historical point of view, and even a glance at the history of the white man will plainly reveal that his development has been technological but not social. He just don't know how to git along with people. All his triumphs and all his happiness deals with things, not people. I believe that

140

white people have different natures than we do. I also believe that we here on this earth to humanize them."

I shook my head. "Man, I don't understand you. I really don't."

"I told you not t'git him started on that stuff," Mojo repeated. "I told you."

Both Ahmad and I ignored him.

Ahmad continued: "Of course you don't understand." He pointed his finger at me. "If you did you wouldn't allow yoself to git hooked up with a white woman. You'd realize that she's yo opposite, and opposites attract each other. Revolution to me is more than just offin the honky. Revolution is change. Our purpose ain't to kill them, it's to change them *without becomin like them,* or even a small part of them, because then we would *be* them. That ain't Nature's plan."

Mojo was really high now. "If you so fuckin smart, how come you ain rich?" He giggled as he drained the last of the whiskey and staggered toward the cupboard to get another bottle.

"Shut up, Mojo," I said. "We serious."

"So's cancer," he called. "For those who got it."

I waved Ahmad to continue.

"Man, he went on, giving Mojo a toothy canine grin, "when you drop a baby in a white chick, you ain't created life the way it was spozed to be, you only destroy an atom in the link of the chain that makes black people strong. You delay the real revolution along with the hopes of the Third World."

I banged my fist on my knee. My voice betrayed my anger and I fought hard to harness them both. "You got some nerve talkin about *hope!*" I shouted. "What you sayin kills all hope —for everybody! I thought our fight was spoze t'be against the rich and the powerful who trample on the poor and needy. It's economic, not racial!"

His voice rose to meet mine. "Well, goddammit, who *is*

the rich and powerful? Who the fuck *is* the poor and needy? Is you tryin to say that all the shit we go through is *economic?* You gotta be outa yo mind! How come—if what you say is true—how come the biggest white racists is the poorest white people: the redneck sharecroppers, the sado cops, the hard-head hardhats and the blue-collar workers—all the mutha-fuckas who ain't got a damn thing more'n us except their dirty white asses? *You tell me that!"*

He immediately calmed down. "Brutha, don't be mad at me for recognizin what is . . . be mad at yoself for not recognizin it."

I *was* mad at myself, damned mad. But not for the reasons he suggested. I was only mad because I wasn't smart enough, I hadn't read enough or given enough time to study it as he had obviously done. Therefore, he and I weren't on equal terms in a debate. Yet, even if my brain was not the storehouse of facts and half-facts that his was, I knew that my gut reaction excelled his ten times over, for all the good that did me.

Mojo just sat with a pot-induced grin on his face; distant, self-satisfied, listening, but through a giant mesh of content-ment that turned all of his bricks of frustration—if he had any —to pabulum.

"I love Terri," I stated. "Why do I love her, Ahmad?"

He looked at me a long time before replying. "It seems that black people is full of love for the things that's responsible for so much of their misery. But what you love is the *idea* of her, and the *idea* of the white boy is what done brainwashed you into believin what love is. What you in love with, is love itself."

"Aw, man, you fulla shit!" I spat out. "You can't tell me what I feel."

"Only because they done already convinced you what you oughta feel—and I'm not tryin to tell you *what* you feel, I'm only tellin you *why* you feel it. Man, they done shot romance into you like a eyedropper fulla heroin. They done gave you movies, where a kiss is always connected with romantic music; they done gave you books, where fuckin is a supernova in the heavenly constellation, and they done gave you television, where neither of these can happen without the use of both a mouthwash and a can of pussy perfume. And all the women you've fantasized about done been white, mostly blonde, and good to look at. Shit, you even think ugly white women is pretty, that's how fucked-up they got us. So you damn right: I can't tell you how you feel. But the tragedy is that neither can you. You don't know nuthin about love, man, all you know is romance—and romance ain't nuthin but true love's trash-can because so many people thrown their garbage into it."

I'd had enough. That cat was too much for me with words. I glanced at my clock and got up, yawned expansively, attempting by my gesture to convey that I was unimpressed, even bored, by the whole conversation.

Ahmad seemed just as unimpressed, but Mojo took my hint. "Man, it's time to split. C'mon, Ahmad. Let's find Cootie befo he do somethin stupid."

Ahmad rose. "Let's hit it. You got any more pot?"

"Naw," Mojo answered. "But we can stop and git some. I know a stud who just got in a batch from Jamaica. Talk about *bad!* You can't smoke a whole joint."

They slapped hands. "Let's make it, then," Ahmad said.

I wasn't about to let them outdo me in nonchalance. "Listen," I said. "I'm layin in all day tomorrow—see if I can git this leg and arm together. Y'all come by next day and I'll lay out the plans I got."

"Okay," they replied together.

They left and I went to lie down. My bravado was gone and my spirit was drained. I thought about my reunion with Terri. It helped. Fuck Ahmad.

14

THERE MUST be someplace in a man's mind where he can go and hide out. I mean, without his being what everyone calls insane. I searched the hell out of mine. I viewed places that I never before knew existed. Thoughts nearly strangled me. Refutations to the things Ahmad had said jumped in and out of my field of vision before I was able to properly focus on them and get them into some semblance of perspective. They slipped away from me piecemeal; I had no real chance to examine them so they made hazy nothingness of all my brainwaves. I tried searching deeper into myself, but all I found was a deeper darkness: a fine place for hiding, but not the least conducive to a thorough search. I needed light and the only light I found anywhere centered around Terri. Everything else seemed hopeless, lost.

Like, was the world really as Ahmad said it was? All I wanted was to make it a better world for everybody. But he said that was his aim, too. So, then, why were we at odds? We were supposed to be soldiers in the same army fighting the same enemy. At least that's the way I'd envisioned our roles. The distance he'd talked about may not, after all, be connected with each individual journey through life—which is what I thought he'd meant—instead it may be only the distance between individual people. It may have to do with our impersonality toward each other, our inability to touch each other without weapons, without the cloak of disinterest that shields us from the contamination we imagine is on the skin of the other. My God, where was the hope?

Love, to Ahmad and millions like him (was I secretly so?) was wrong by virtue of being given to someone whose skin was of another hue. My mind screamed to find the sense in that. I mean, for instance, I knew many light black people—lighter than whites—who had jet-black mates. Why wasn't their relationship wrong, too? What, in the name of everything holy, made the difference . . . and why couldn't I have asked these questions while he and I had been talking?

In a way, however, he had given an answer when he'd spouted that junk about putting a baby into a white chick weakens the Third World; but, damn it, most of the Third World was light-skinned! (I could clearly imagine him saying "That's why they were weak in the first place.")

A heavy sorrow climbed over my body. I downed whiskey like it was water. I tore the bandages from my wounds and poured liquor over them as though it was a purification ritual. I don't know why. I don't know. I got up and paced the floor; a chair was in my way. Instead of moving it I picked it up and slammed it against the wall, breaking it and knocking another large piece of plaster to the floor. I stared into my red bulb and watched the world bleed. Like Jesus, life was being crucified—and for the same reasons.

Finally I sat up and, being unable to hold on any longer, I cried. I mean real tears, too. I cried for America, for its brash, unfulfilled promises; for all the hopes it had trampled and squashed into the grimy mud of its country roads and its streamlined superhighways. I cried because it tore, without mercy, the very bonds that were meant to hold people together. I cried for Terri and I cried for Ahmad; I wept bitterly for the Ku Klux Klan and B'Nai B'Rith; I died in Mississippi and Viet Nam; shed tears for President Nixon and Martin Luther King. Most of all I cried for myself.

When tears would no longer come I sat on my sofa and thought of pure, clean murder. Murder without reason, murder because all hope was, in the end, hopeless. And I wanted to cry some more.

I had to get out into the streets. I had to do something or I would've gone raving mad. I put on my shoes and jacket and headed for Spoon's where I knew I'd find a sane insensibility because the people didn't give a damn who you were so long as you didn't fuck-up the party.

The night was a comfortable flurry of small breezes and winking stars when I stepped out of my miserable pad. People were out in force (I'd forgotten, in my gloom, that it was the weekend). It was a good night for walking and my leg was feeling good. The exercise would be good for it.

On the way downtown I stopped at Wesley's Bar. I don't know why, because I seldom went in the place. The atmosphere was a bit too heady for my taste. I mean, so many of its patrons were those gnomes from City Hall who looked down on guys like me—unless we dressed in suits and ties. Then they couldn't gauge what our occupation was. If you looked as though you worked in an office they became right nice people. The place was also frequented by councilmen, assemblymen, lawyers, cops (in civvies, of course) and a variety of that new breed, new-monied Poverty Executive: poverty pimps (who were well aware of the secretaries, receptionists, file-clerks and secret prostitutes that came to the bar trying to latch onto security by latching on to one of them). The men usually got what they wanted: sex. The women almost always got what they didn't want: the gate, when sex was done. It was a good place in which to watch phonies who at least had some style. And in watching their agonied attempts at sophistication one could very easily forget one's own troubles.

Business was at full blast when I entered. The music was soft and the barmaid, Be-bop Betty, handled the demanding customers with a gentle ease, though she really had her work cut out for her. Most of them wanted fancy, mixed drinks even though at any other bar they would be drinking beer.

Dressed in one of his sharp sport coats, Wesley played the genial host to people he didn't particularly like, while his common-law wife, Big Momma Sandora, sat at the end of the bar (her customary seat) and kept a wary eye on the cash register. If Be-bop Betty placed a dime in the register's penny box, Big Momma was sure to notice where it had been mis-placed to, and Wesley would be sure to hear about it later. Big Momma was a good woman to have around and Wesley knew it. No matter how good-looking other women might be —and many were—they'd have a hard time getting Wesley away from Big Momma. Quite a few had tried and failed.

I ordered one drink while I observed Bow-wow Charlie get-ting drunk in order to build his nerve for his oft-repeated rou-tine: he'd make dates with two or more women ("insurance" he called it) expecting one not to show up. If they all showed up he'd get drunk and tell them all to go to hell. The one that didn't get insulted and leave would be his companion for the rest of the evening.

I slowly sipped at my drink, watching with growing interest

the emotional games people were playing with each other. It was fun, but my interest faded sooner than it usually did. I decided to continue on to Spoon's where the phonies were of my own caliber.

Just as I was leaving I heard Don, one of the poverty intellectuals, say to a woman he'd been closely eyeing, "Pardon me, sister. I've been observing you. There's something about you . . . What's your astrological sign?"

That was his game. If the woman was interested in that sign junk (Don really wasn't), she'd find herself with her thighs propped open for him tomorrow evening after he'd taken her to dinner. He seldom failed.

I smiled and walked out. I think it was the first time I'd smiled since I'd seen Terri.

So many people were dancing when I got to Spoon's that the floor shook and caused a slight twinge of pain in my leg. I took the first available seat.

"My man!" Spoon shouted at me above the music and the loud laughter. "What's happ'nin, baby? Ain't seen you but once since you won the Champeenship!"

"Hey, Spoon-o!" I called back, trying hard to match his jocularity. "I been gittin it t'gether, man. How you been?"

"Man, I'm beatin the dogs to the garbage cans—but just barely. Whacha havin t'drink?"

"Gimme some Grand-Dad and Coke."

"Right on!" He bounced away to fix my drink.

None of my troops were in the place. I was glad of it, too, because I had told them I was going to lay in until day after tomorrow. If they saw me out now they might begin to think I was unreliable or something. Like, if they needed me they had the right to expect me to be where I said I'd be, instead of someplace jiving around.

Lillian, the prettiest woman to frequent Spoon's, came over to me. I mean, the chick just left her dance partner right in the middle of the floor and walked over to me like she was my woman, or something. The guy kept right on dancing; didn't even seem to notice that she was gone. I guess that's one of the greatest values of the modern dances: never a moment's embarrassment.

"Hi, baby," she cooed. "How's the fightinest nigga in town?" She was a little high.

"Hello, foxy lady," I smiled. "How you?"

"Wanna dance with me?" she asked, attempting to pull me up.

"Sorry, baby. Can't. Got my leg messed up the other day."

"Oh, yeah," she dropped my hands as if her very touch caused me excruciating pain. "I heard about that. I'm sorry, baby," she ended sincerely.

"Ain't nuthin," I assured her. She turned to leave but I grabbed her hands this time. "Hey, uh, where'd you hear about my leg?"

She looked surprised. "Why, Cootie told me. He told everybody. Shit, made you out to be better than Jesse James."

"He was in here, huh?" I was trying hard to hold back my exasperation at Cootie. But I felt a secret joy that she was aware of my exploits.

"He just left a little while ago," she told me.

Spoon sat my drink down on the bar.

"Hey Spoon!" Lillian called. "Wasn't Cootie just in here? How long ago he leave?"

"Bout fifteen minutes," Spoon answered. He turned to go, then looked at me closely, snapping his fingers and pointing to me. *"Oh, yeah!* The drink's on the house, my man. Help heal yo wounds."

I nodded a thank you as he moved back down the bar. Then I turned to Lillian, who was gently massaging my hands. "What'd Cootie say happened?" I wanted to know.

"Said y'all was pullin some kinda big job when shootin

started and you and him had t'jump outa a second-story window and you got cut by flyin glass. Said he didn cause he knew how to fall. He bought the whole bar a drink, too."

"Thanks, momma," I said. "Have one on me, too." I gestured to Spoon, who wasted no time getting to me—probably thought I'd do the same thing Cootie had done.

"One—for her," I ordered.

I watched Lillian take her drink and bump back out onto the dance floor, sloshing liquor as she went and laughing stridently when some of it ruined her partner's shined shoes.

Well, I had been correct, Cootie was the one doing the talking, the big mouth. I hoped Ahmad and Mojo would soon find him.

The music temporarily halted and another girl came over to me. I guess she'd seen me buy the drink for Lillian. What I thought until she said, "Kin I have my seat back?" was that she wanted one too.

"Oh! Sure." I said, easing from the stool after offering an apology.

"S'alright," she replied curtly and sat down with her back to me. I didn't know her anyway. Some of the broads who came to Spoon's thought they were too cute.

I left the place without saying anything to anyone. The night was fairly quiet except for the passing of an occasional car. Some Puerto Ricans were standing on the corner as I passed, waiting for a bus. One of them had a radio and I heard the vibrant strains of *Oyé como va* throwing rhythms to the stars. The music made me feel better and I walked on a little lighter for having heard it.

I had walked all the way up to Springfield Avenue, a distance of nearly two miles, before I realized how far I'd come. I hadn't been aware because my head had been filled with my earlier conversation with Ahmad. I didn't want the kind of world he envisaged. But neither did I want the one in which I was forced to function. The one I wanted didn't seem to exist anywhere but within the confines of my little, dingy apartment while I was in the arms of my forbidden love—the seemingly greatest impracticality of all because it was the only one real enough to be totally impossible to achieve in peace. I resolved that I'd have a talk with Terri tomorrow. I had to get myself straightened out somehow.

15

I TOLD her the truth, the entire truth, everything: The gang and my involvement with them, the beating of Vito, the robbery, the girls I had, my talk with Ahmad, and even my indecisiveness concerning her and me. She had listened patiently as it tumbled from my mouth like a runaway river. Her emotions were only betrayed by the amount of cigarettes she smoked and the tight, white lines that formed around her mouth.

After she'd heard it and I'd ended by asking for her help, for her to try and understand what I was going through, her voice was a study of controlled passion.

"I'm not sure I can. I don't know if I can understand or help you; and the only real help lies within you. You have to choose, and it's going to be hard."

"But the choice involves you as much as it do me, don't it?"

"No," she said. "Not necessarily. I know what I am. I'm a bleeding-heart liberal. The kind who shies away from dangerous involvement, whose liberalism is for distant atrocities. I know that much about myself. What I feel for a starving child, or a pathetic junkie, has nothing to do with how I'll act in a given situation."

"I thought it would be different with me," I said dejectedly.

"It is, darling, but the dilemma is *yours;* I *know* what I want. Those people have my pity—my guilt, if you will. And I will always be able to forgive them for their weaknesses, for allowing themselves to be kicked in the teeth or destroyed by a power greater than themselves. But how could I ever forgive your power to destroy me? Don't you see? It's really not up to me to understand you so much as it is for you to understand me . . . the both of us. They have my pity, but you control my passion.

She sounded quite *un*impassioned to me. I felt physical pain that had nothing to do with my wounds. It was, I knew, from the effort to explain adequately enough to her what was going on inside me. There seemed no way for me to get across to anybody lately.

She was certainly not giving me any help. "That's just it; I don't know what's right anymore. You right, Ahmad's right—it seems that every-fuckin-body is right but me!"

Terri lit a smoke while I poured myself a drink. This was the only time we'd been alone together that I had not given lovemaking the most prominent place in my thoughts. My despair consumed my energies, leaving no room to pleasure-trip. I felt empty of emotion, except for the huge dose of self-pity in which I wallowed like a pig in shit.

She let out a long stream of smoke. "I can't help you. Even if I could I wouldn't, because this is your decision and yours alone. If I dared force you one way or the other you'd still never be really sure that you did the right thing. You'd feel that you copped-out, and you'd blame me." She held up her hand to stave off my protest.

"Don't say you wouldn't," she went on. "On the other hand, if you became what you say, a leader of your people, there'd always be some Ahmads around to put you down for talking black and sleeping white. No matter what sacrifices you might make, I'd be the millstone around your neck, your stigma, your patch of leprosy, and, therefore, your most vulnerable weakness. Because of me you'd have to prove your blackness to the world every day. Do you love me enough for that? *Don't answer!* Don't even try, because I love you too much to be the cause of your having to prove it. I won't allow you to make my love an instrument of your destruction. I love you for what you are, not for what you think you have to be."

I looked at her, not understanding what she meant. Why couldn't I just say fuck Ahmad and everybody who thought as he did? Hadn't I proved myself to them? They started out my tormentors and ended up my followers. Did I expect the world to do the same as a greater proof?

I had already defied the boundaries, hadn't I? I had fucked one of their forbidden women, I had beaten up one of their lordly men, I had broken their sacred laws. What else did I need? Perhaps I needed for them to know.

"What am I, Terri? I mean, what am I—to you?" I asked.

She seemed mildly put out by the question. Finally, she said, "You're the man I love, that's what you are. How deep it goes is unknown. I want you more than practically anything."

"But you don't want me at all costs, do you?" I was pushing.

She gave me a searching look, yet I saw in the back of her eyes a plea that begged me not to push farther into a direction

154

she wasn't prepared to travel with me. Her tongue darted nervously over her lips.

"Do you expect an answer? Really? How can I answer a question like that?" She seemed close to tears. "How?"

"As truthfully as you can," I said coldly. "Can you accept me as the leader of a bunch of guys who might hate you enough to kill you? Can you accept me as a possible destroyer of people because they have the same skin color you got? Can you accept me as a robber? A mugger? A deliberate liar?"

"*Why?*" she yelled shrilly. "Why should I have to?"

"Because I'm a man who done fell in love with his sense of being. Baby, listen to me! For a while I was nuthin in this neighborhood—a big, fat *nuthin* working in a factory. But now, when I walk down the streets, or into a bar, I git me some *respect. Respect!* You hear that? You know what that means? Dig it. People who chased me now wanna follow me. Guys wanna buy me drinks, women wanna gimme pussy, and kids wanna grow up t'be like me. *Respect!* You accepted the passive, workin punk. Can you accept the *man?* I wanna know how deep it go, Terri."

"To me, the guy you call a punk *was* the man," she said very softly.

Her face was so soft now. Her voice whispered, "Oh, my darling. Please. For *our* sakes, don't get caught up and trapped in petty self-importance. Look at what happens to those who do. Where are all those fine young firebrands of the nineteen sixties? *Where are they?* Love me, darling. Love me and let me love you!"

She held onto my hands as if trying to hold onto my former self. I felt her trembling and watched the tears well in her eyes with such anxiety that a lump began to form in my throat. I felt my heart racing to pump the blood through my excited body. I felt her anguish deeply. I was profoundly moved by the signs of her caring.

"You still didn't answer my question, Terri?"

She buried her head in my lap while I fought back the urge to take her in my arms and comfort her. But I had to know how deep went her commitment to me.

"Please," she cried. "Please don't play games with me. Don't do this to us."

I held fast. "You didn't answer. Can you accept me as I am?"

She spoke so softly and yet with such a determined tone that I wasn't sure I heard her say "no" until she raised her head and looked at me through her red-rimmed eyes. "No," she repeated quietly. "Because you're not like you think you are."

I felt like I'd been banged in the chest by a blow from the powerful arm of Ruben "Hurricane" Carter. My breath stopped and my senses reeled before my eyes like a mad, uncontrollable Ferris Wheel.

"You don't mean that," I croaked.

"I *do* mean it. Yes," she sobbed. "I *must* mean it, or else we'll grow to hate each other. It'll shatter and destroy you most, and I'll be unable to help, and that'll destroy me also. Oh, don't you see, my darling? *Can't* you see?"

"What we gon do, then?" I asked as calmly as I could. But looking at her only brought "Hurricane" Carter's devastating fist smashing into me again.

She rose and stood before me, her own sense of pride making her back stiffen. "I don't know. I'll have to leave it up to you. I guess we both need to do some serious thinking."

I nodded in agreement. She turned away and walked toward the toilet to fix her make-up. It didn't take but a few minutes, and when she came out she announced that she was ready to go home.

She tried to object when I offered to walk her to the taxi-stand, but I overrode her—maybe out of a last, vain attempt at hope, the hope that we could, somehow, work something out before we reached our destination. We walked the entire distance in a dismal silence.

The cab had pulled off before I realized that I should have made love to her one last futile time.

16

I WASN'T about to go home. All I'd do there would be to brood, feel sorry for myself, and wind up calling Terri to give away my manhood to her woman's fear. So I walked and thought. Tried to sort things out and put them in their proper place. But nothing went in its proper place, ever. Everything was decidedly out of joint—including me. I felt alienated from everything and everybody.

People waved at me and spoke to me, but I failed to recognize them. My hands were jammed into my pockets and my eyes only lifted from the cruddy ground to give me direction. And I had no idea where I was going. The hardest thing in the world at that moment would have been to tell anyone where I was headed.

I stopped at Belmont Avenue and stood looking at the vast

empty lots of broken brick and smashed plaster, the dismal refuse of urban renewal. Nothing was renewed. Black windows of the few remaining empty houses stared back at me. We both saw nothing.

It was Sunday. Many people had to meet the Man on Monday so the streets were free of their usual stragglers. Enough people, however, were out so that one didn't have to be lonely. I felt as though some deep chasm had opened up and that no one could hear my tiny voice crying in the darkness, and nobody cared to unless I gave in to their demands upon my soul. Devils, all. But for me the devils broke up into two camps and screamed their demands at me, not knowing or caring that true recognition of the real me would bring drastic changes, pleasant, too, upon them. But neither camp was prepared to change.

I headed up Fifteenth Avenue, aimlessly wandering in mind and body. I was near Bergen Street. Since I was up this far I thought that I might as well drop in and have a drink at Ted Hardy's new place. I liked Ted because he was a hustler nobody could stop no matter how much they put him down with their bad-mouthing. He always bounced back—and provided jobs for those same fools whenever he opened a new bar.

"BAM!" A shot? *"BLAMmmm!"* A shot.

I hit the ground fast behind a parked car. I didn't know where the shots had come from or at whom they were directed, and I was afraid to look up and find out. A picture of Vito and the Mafia jumped into my mind. Were they gunning for me?

I heard a woman cry out in pain about a block away. I won't lie. Relief flowed into me. I jumped up, knowing that no one was shooting at me, to hear a man's bitter upbraiding voice shouting:

"What the fuck you do that for? She wasn't doin nuthin but

talkin! You spoze t'be a po-lice officer! you dirty cocksuka! Shoot me! Whyn't you shoot me, too?"

I ran toward the commotion. About twenty people were there already and more were gathering. One cop was bending over the woman, who lay moaning on the littered sidewalk, while the other cop, a man handcuffed standing beside him, was trying to disperse the crowd.

"You people back away!" he yelled. "Come on, break it up and g'wan home!" His gun was in his hand and his eyes literally glittered with the fear and excitement within him. The man beside him, handcuffed with his hands behind him, kept up a torrent of profanity ending always with the question: "What the hell you shoot her for?"

"Shut up, you!" the cop kept saying. But it was plain to see that his mind, like his eyes, was on that angry, growing crowd.

"Ain't that JoAnn Eason?" a woman asked.

"Yeah," someone answered. "That muthafuckin cracka pig shot her down like a dog!"

"She sho look in a bad way . . ."

"I seen the whole thang," somebody else volunteered. "That child ain't done *nuthin*. He shot her f'nuthin!"

The handcuffed man picked up on that. "Be my witness!" he shouted to the unknown voice. "Anybody who seen it, please be my witness!" He broke into loud, body-shaking sobs, but between them he went on cursing at the cop holding him. "Dirty, white sombitch! You shot my woman f'nuthin! *F'nuthin!"*

Several people in the crowd came forward and volunteered to be his witnesses, but I don't think he even heard them. Most of them faded back to the fringes, not caring to get involved.

One man said, "Man, I can't be no witness t'nuthin. My ol lady got warrants out on me for nonsupport."

Another whispered: "I got traffic warrants. Shit, I go down-town t'witness, dey throw me *under* the jail-house. I ain't takin my black ass *no*where!"

Two junkies backed away in favor of a fix. A wino waved his partner away with a full bottle of Boone's Farm Apple wine.

The cop kneeling over the woman took out his handker-chief and wiped his wet brow and said, "She's a goner, Eddie. Better call in."

The handcuffed man's wail echoed down the block. The crowd roared its grief, and general confusion prevailed. The handcuffed man dropped to his knees and sobbed out his sor-row on the dead woman's breast.

"Baby!" he cried. "Jo, *baby."* He was trying to call her back to life. "Honey, *don't* die! Honey, *don't* leave me! Oh, good *God!"* He raised his wet face to the skies. It was a mask of wretched pain. "My Lawd! Give her back to me! *Give my baby back to me!"*

The skies remained silent and he put his head back upon her lifeless breast, moaning woefully.

The Eddie-cop didn't know what to do. He stood confused, above the weeping man, not even realizing that he was waving his gun about like an idiot. He appeared to want to laugh and cry at the same time, depending upon which notion reached his befuddled brain first: Was she alive? Was she dead?

His partner finally took Eddie-cop's gun hand and guided the weapon to its holster while Eddie-cop verged on hysteria.

"Go call in, Eddie!" the other cop shouted twice before Eddie took his first tentative steps toward the patrol car. He stumbled to it looking bewildered and dazed.

"What happened?" a newcomer asked.

"Them muthafuckas done killed JoAnn!" a heavy-set woman replied.

"Whut!" the newcomer exclaimed. "You mean she sho-*nuff* dead, good-lookin as she is?"

"What the fuck you think she mean, you dumb bastard!" That was my voice I heard say that. I hadn't intended it. It came out before I thought.

"Don't git mad at *me,* man," the newcomer said. "I jes axed whut happened."

I wasn't mad at him, but I know it sounded as though I was; I didn't know what I was feeling, yet I found myself saying: "Go ask that goddamn pig over there what happened." I pointed at the cop to make sure he knew, for him and the cop, who I meant.

The cop was only about ten feet away from me. He started toward me in what appeared to be slow motion. His mouth was moving below his red, angry eyes, but the anger I felt fulminating inside me deafened me so that all I could hear was the harshness of my own breathing.

The cop stopped in front of me and it seemed like I could smell the hate, fear and body odor emanating from his sweaty, blue shirt. The scent assailed my nostrils and stoked the boiling in my gut.

"If you ain't a witness, fella," he spoke into my face, "ya better move out. G'wan home."

"Fuck you!" I seethed at him.

He looked genuinely shocked. "What'd you say?" he asked as though his hearing had failed him.

"I said fuck you," I repeated loudly. "We live in this dump. *You* go home." I hadn't really thought consciously to antagonize him, really, but I looked at that dead woman and her grieving man and I just couldn't contain the hostility inside me. My brain told my mouth to be quiet, but my mouth simply disobeyed.

"Yeah, you go home, you fuckin pig!" somebody from the crowd yelled.

The cop didn't take his attention from me. "You wanna get locked up for incitin a riot?" he warned.

"Kiss my black ass!" I shot back at him. And even then, with my rage tearing me apart and leaping up to engulf me wholly, I wondered why I was doing what I was doing, and why I could think of nothing but curse words to say to him.

"One more word, buddy, and you've *had* it!" He backed away with his gun hand hanging loosely at his side.

I was about to give him that one more word when the handcuffed man raised up. He took the few steps over to where the cop and I were having our standoff.

"Mistah," he addressed the cop. "Why y'all kill my woman? We wuz only arguin. Why y'all hada kill her?"

"She had a knife, didn't she?" the cop yelled at him. "How'd we know what she was gonna do?"

"But she wasn comin after y'all." The man could hardly get the words out. "She jes took it from me t'keep me from fightin a guy in the bar, that's all . . . she wasn't tryin t'harm y'all. She only . . ."

I could barely stand to look at the man. His throat had swelled to half again its size. He struggled for words, but they just wouldn't come. He grimaced with his mouth open, and tears spilled over to mix with the mucus that ran freely from his nose along with the saliva foaming at the corners of his mouth. It was a tragic, horrible sight. He looked so forlorn, so lost and so terrible. He was like a moronic child, and so very ugly in his sadness.

But when I realized that his hands were manacled behind his back, that he couldn't help himself, he became, for me, instantly as beautiful as a painting of the African prince Chaka that Terri had shown me in a book by J. A. Rogers. His beauty expanded, swift and clean. I wanted to hug him and give him what comfort I could.

He kept trying for communication. Eyes that saw all tried

to speak to the cop. But the cop only averted his sneering face so as not to get sprayed by the liquid anguish of the man. He held him at arm's length.

Words were lost. The man's vocal cords simply wouldn't work. He kept trying and failing and the cop got impatient.

Suddenly the man shrieked out the most terrifyingly painful sound I'd ever heard. It wasn't anything like a human voice. It would have made a banshee sound like a robin by comparison. His mouth opened and I could have sworn that it was filled with dragon fire, though I'm sure it was only the neon and street lights reflected in the immense amount of human fluid that had covered the man's mouth and head.

Then, so quickly that no one had a chance to move, the man bent low and charged the cop. He hit him very hard right in the stomach.

The cop was knocked into me and I in turn into others behind me. We all must have looked like human dominoes going down from the playful finger of a child.

I heard many screams as we toppled and I heard whoops of pure joy. I also heard the tough cop cry out: *"Oh, Mother of God! Save me!"*

His voice had undergone a marked change. He'd started out a bass and ended up a soprano. I smiled at the sissy in him when his badge of authority disappeared.

I climbed from under a pack of people in time to see the handcuffed man kicking the cop in the face, in the body and everywhere else he found an opening. He had remarkable balance, no doubt inspired by his instinct to kill that which had killed a part of him.

Eddie-cop—recovered from his initial shock, but about to have conniptions this time—came running toward the crowd firing his gun into the air.

"Awright, hold it! Everybody freeze!" He was yelling at the

top of his voice but nobody froze for him. He had a momentary attack of indecision, but got over it quickly and came rushing on.

I saw him point his gun at the handcuffed man, who was still kicking the downed cop. Mass confusion prevailed. He might have shot into the crowd and hit any number of people, but, somehow, I got the distinct impression that Eddie-cop could hit what he wanted with little trouble.

I pulled the handcuffed man down just in time, because the bullet zinged over his head, missing him by inches. It would have splattered his brains over everywhere had I been a second slower in spilling him to the ground.

Eddie-cop was about to fire again when the heavy-set lady that I'd noticed before bumped him so hard that he dropped his weapon.

"Come on, man!" I shouted into the handcuffed man's ear. He didn't even hear me. I don't even think he knew what was happening. He was spitting at the cop and moving toward him. When he got to the fallen man, despite my trying to pull him away, he growled like a wild animal.

He buried his head in the cop's lap. The cop was either out cold or dead, I don't know which. But the handcuffed man grunted and began rooting like a hog in the cop's lap. It took me a full minute to pull his head away. I got him to his feet, listening to his madness while at the same time looking around for Eddie-cop and hoping I didn't get shot. I finally saw him struggling out from beneath the heavy-set woman and looking around for his gun, which I couldn't see.

"Man, you better come on here! Let's git outa here!"

I still hadn't looked at him because suddenly all the noise of the crowd ceased. It got so quiet that I was sure I'd turn to look into the muzzle of a national guardsman's carbine that would blow me a brand-new asshole.

But there was nothing behind me. No cops or tanks. Yet everyone seemed to be looking my way, their faces alive with torturous amazement. I checked myself out quickly, then I looked at the handcuffed man. I nearly got sick. His face was a great mass of blood, and he was grinning. He was still grunting too, making those same hog sounds he'd been making while we were on the ground, and now I saw the reason for them.

His mouth was smeared with blood and flesh, and it ran down the front of the man's clothing. He stood there next to me. I fought back my nausea and forced myself to look at the barren hole in the front of the cop's blue pants.

But now Eddie-cop had recovered and was coming toward us, cursing wildly with tears of stark horror raining down upon his cheeks.

"*Savage nigger bastards!*" he screamed. I realized that he meant me too. "I'm gonna kill ya! If it's the last thing I do, I'm gonna *kill* ya! You'll be deader'n that nigger whore when I get ya!"

I snatched the handcuffed man and went running with him down Springfield Avenue with panic gripping my head in a steel vise. I only looked back once, and I saw Eddie-cop picking up his fallen comrade's gun. He began firing at us and I didn't look back anymore.

By some stroke of luck—or Eddie-cop's blind fury—we made the corner. I was grateful that that was when the handcuffed man chose to fall down.

"You shot?" I wheezed.

"Naw, I ain't shot," he said. That grin was still on his face.

I pulled at him. "Well, then git the fuck up. We gotta move!"

He was laughing—*laughing!*—spitting out blood, his face a crisscrossed map of scars and knife wounds.

"Don't you spit that shit my way," I warned.

"Where we goin, man?" He said it like he didn't have a care in the world.

I drew a total blank. Didn't have the slightest idea where we were going, or even where we could go. I considered running off and leaving him, until I thought about his dead woman lying a mere block away from us.

"We gotta git the hell away from here first," I said.

We started running down Belmont Avenue until we reached West Kinney Street. I heard a siren wailing off in the distance. I wasn't about to take this dude to my house, nor was I going to go there myself. Then I remembered that I knew damn near everybody living in the Kinney Street projects, any one of whom would gladly take us in. *Us!* What the hell was I talking about, "us"? I glanced at the awkward figure running beside me. Yes, I suppose it would have to be that way: us, us, us. Here was this dude I didn't even know an hour ago, had never seen before, and he'd just made a decision for me that I'd probably adhere to for the rest of my life. Each beat of our feet on the pavement proclaimed *us.*

"How you feel about guerrilla warfare against the pigs, man?" I asked.

Breathlessly he said, "Open warfare'd be more to my taste, brutha-man. But I'll take what I can git."

My troops had been crying for action, I thought. Well, they'd better be really ready. I wondered if they were. The sirens were coming closer. We picked up speed. The projects were near and I was sure we'd make them now.

Terri's face suddenly loomed before me. It was clear in all its details. She smiled at me and her hand went up to flick away a stray hair. My steps faltered and my chest began to ache. I came dangerously close to falling flat on my face, but I quickly recovered.

My mind began to fade her out. Not without sadness, and certainly not without a great sense of loss. I labored to hold the picture for just a moment longer.

I should have made love to her for the last time.

The closer I got to the projects the more her image faded until another blast of that siren erased it completely. I kissed what was left of her cheek in my mind, then I finally let her go altogether.

I looked over at my running-mate and visualized a picture of his lifeless woman, lying on the cold ground with her blood spilling out in a deep red pool.

"What's yo name, man?" I asked.